I0570853

Summer's Hollow
By Samantha Curtin

1

Published by
Behind the Curtin Publications
8931 Early April Way
Columbia, MD 21046

Curtin, Samantha
Summer's Hollow
ISBN 978-0-615-80486-6

The text of this book is set in 12-point Times New Roman

Book Design by Samantha Curtin

Prologue

Mary took a deep breath, swept the blonde hair from her face, and walked up the wooden steps to the large oak front door. Her arm extended forward to grasp the bronze knob but it never quite made it. Instead, it hovered somewhere in between as she looked up at the structure of the house. The wooden monolith was perched at the edge of the woods. It seemed to tower over everything, even the trees around it that stood taller.

The sinking feeling in the pit of Mary's stomach was almost too much to bear as her pale hand firmly grasped the knob. It turned ever so slowly in her palm and eventually made way for the door to creak open. The sound of it seemed to echo around the foyer and she prayed that Edward had not heard her come in. She wanted nothing more than to gather up all her things and get out of this hell.

She crept into the house on the balls of her feet and quietly shut the heavy door behind her. Silence was loud in her ears as she looked around for any sign of Edward. After the coast was clear she continued her silent journey up the stairs and into the bedroom. There was still no sign that Edward was home and she let out a sigh of relief. Hastily, she pulled out her bag from under the peach bed skirt and started to shove anything she could fit into it.

The hairs on the back of her neck stood up as she went to buckle her bag closed. Every part of her was screaming not to turn around so instead she slowly stood up, collecting her bag. Then out of nowhere a great force hit her and she was thrust into the wall. She dropped the bag in her hands as her face was smashed into the wall. The wallpaper scratched her soft, pale cheeks as she felt a hot breath on her neck and a hand going up her dress.

"Sweetie, are you going somewhere?" came that horrid voice in her ear.

She struggled against him, not speaking a word. He kissed her neck as he still had her pinned up against the wall. This was the very thing that she was trying to escape from: the constant rapes and beatings. Her mind tried to shut down like it usually did but then something in her snapped. That stench and feel of him all over her was enough to make her hurl. Mixed in with the nausea was a white hot rage. This rage was enough to drive her to shove back at Edward knocking him away.

"Mary, dear," he said with an eerie calmness as she turned around to face him, "What do you think you're doing?"

"I'm leaving, Edward…" she forced the words out.

He laughed. He tilted back his head, grabbed his stomach and laughed. It echoed around the room and in her ears. She cringed at this display but used this distraction to start towards the door. His hand grasped her neck as the laughing abruptly stopped. Instead it was replaced by the cold stare of his soulless grey eyes. They looked down inside of her, trying to scare out any of the rage that flooded her right now.

Mary sputtered to breathe as she slammed her hands into his arm over and over trying to knock him loose. All she succeeded in doing was turning him on even more. He threw her onto the bed, throat still in hand. His cold hand once again slid up her dress, little did he know that was the last time he would ever do that. Her rage peaked as she slid her hand under her pillow and withdrew a knife.

Her head swam as his hand still pressed against her throat but she was aware enough to see where his head was. In one move she drove the knife deep into the side of his neck. Those grey eyes held a look of surprise as he let out a loud yell and fumbled

4

around for the knife. She quickly moved off of the bed as he tried to pull the knife out, blood running everywhere. Now it was her turn to smash his face up against that wall.

Blood ran down her hands as she pulled the knife out of his neck as he now sputtered and groped his way to the wall. Skin came loose with the blade as if she had sliced a piece of meat from the bone. It became smashed against the rough wallpaper as she used her already bloody forearm to push his limp body against that wall that she was all too familiar with. The sound of him gurgling on his own blood made her laugh. The sound slipped from her lips and was foreign to her. That sound gave her the will to finish the act she had started.

Those grey eyes rolled back in his head as his body began to twitch. A pool of blood was collecting by the wall as the flesh was slowly creeping down like a raindrop on a window. She allowed his body to also slide down the wall and gather in a pile on the floor. He was still alive, still breathing, and that was a problem for her. The knife was held firmly in her right hand, dripping blood on the floor as the rage fully manifested itself. It turned this poor defenseless woman into the powerful witch that lurked deep down.

Blood cascaded through the air as she swiftly shoved the knife up and into Edward's eye. What little strength he had left was used to utter a cry that sounded as if it were underwater. Thick, deep red blood poured over her hand as she still held the knife. The last movement of his body was to lurch forward and dive into the pool of his own blood. Those cold hands, those cold eyes, and that horrid voice would never bother her again.

5

For what seemed like hours, she stood there staring down at the gory scene. Her pale skin was now red with his blood. It all became very real to her and her eyes opened wide with fright. The rage had passed and the fear was back. Her chest ached as she quickly tried to wipe the blood off on her red dress. It was a lost cause.

Instead she carefully picked up her bag that the pool of blood was extending its crimson wave towards. It was a moot point trying to avoid getting the blood from her skin on the bag so she quickly scooped it up and charged out of the house. Her heart was beating hard in her chest as she was afraid Judith would come home and find her covered in blood. There was no time to clean up; she just rushed out the door before she had time to wrap her head around what she had done.

The wind was picking up as she took off down the dirt road towards the woods. She fought through the trees and underbrush while she kept looking over her shoulder. The feeling that someone was following her grew with intensity the deeper she went into the forest. The trees above her creaked and swayed as if mocking her. They seemed to go on forever as her bag became heavy in her hands.

A twig snapped behind her but when she whirled her head around she found nothing. Darkness grew in the woods as she found herself now approaching the cemetery that sat on the edge. This meant that she was closer to the town. Then it struck her. Where was she going? She was so hell bent on getting out of there that she hadn't formulated a plan to what her destination was. The anxiety in her chest increased to the point where she had to stop and catch her breath; her body had to pick the cemetery to do this of course.

Her bag fell to the moss covered ground with a dull thud. The blonde hair that was once neatly pulled back into a barrette was now a sweaty, frizzy mess around her face. She reached her hand up to push some of the frizz back but stopped as she saw the blood caked on her hands. The thought of what had happened back at the house suddenly hit her hard. It was enough to knock her to her knees.

There she knelt, on the moss covered stone walkway of the cemetery, clutching her chest with her blood stained hands. That sick feeling was creeping into her throat and she feared she would lose the contents of her stomach all over the smooth stones. She shut her eyes quickly, her fingers clawing at the lace lining of her dress trying to catch her breath. Eventually she was on all fours panting like a dog in heat. Her panting quickly stopped as she heard a sobering sound: the clip clopping of heels on the stones.

Her breathing stopped all together and her eyes grew wide. She turned to see the hem of a dark maroon dress and black heeled boots. Each step closer made the mass in her throat rise. Every part of her told her to run, to flee as far away from this woman as possible but she couldn't move. Frozen in fear, Mary heard the shoes stop right by her side. Against every fiber of her being her head turned on its own to look up at the towering figure above her.

Judith was haloed by the stone archway of the cemetery. Her lip quivered and her nose scrunched as if she had something unpleasant underneath it. Mary's heart was beating so fast that it cued her panting again/all over again/once more. Fear was wide in her eyes as Judith's quivering lipped curled into a sneer. The scene then faded into nothing as everything went black.

Chapter 1- The Long Walk

The cool wind was strong as it guided Rylie to the cemetery that loomed at the edge of the woods. A storm was on its way, blotting out the growing light of the morning. She came to the stone arch of the cemetery and stopped as she eyed the moss covered stones above her with reproach. Even in the dim sunlight, it sent chills down her spine with its stones that had fallen off in chunks, littering the walkway below it. She looked back at her farm house at the bottom of the hill; she could hardly see it through the thick cluster of trees around the entrance of the cemetery.

After a deep breath and much internal coaxing, she stepped onto the rough stones and made her way through the overgrown grass. At first she walked fast but then she started to jog. She heard a rustling noise behind her and this caused her to pick up her pace to a run. The noise stopped as she breathed heavily and stood still at the edge of a small grave. A hand clamped down on her shoulder; she screamed loudly and jumped. Someone chuckled behind her and she whirled around to see Sarah standing there grinning.

"Jumpy today, aren't we? Oh wait . . . you're always like that." She snickered.

"You know this cemetery freaks me out! Don't do that again." Sarah started to open her mouth again, but Rylie took her by the hand and ran. "We'll talk after we're out."

Rylie and Sarah rushed through the cemetery, careful not to trip over any of the gravestones or loose soil. They came to the clearing on the other side and Rylie breathed a sigh of relief and exhaustion. They continued to walk along the worn path through the thick, tall grass of the small field.

"So what are you doing tomorrow?" Rylie asked as she tugged some stray grass out of her brown hair that was pulled to the side in a thick braid.

Sarah squinted and titled her head in confusion, "Well I'm going to school, then going home, then. . . ."

"No, no. I mean for Bloody Friday."

"Oh come on, Rye, you know I don't do that stuff. It's all made up"

"How can you not believe in it?" Rylie retorted. "I mean the story is real - we have evidence of it in the town for crying out loud!"

"Rye, let's look at the facts here. We have a supposed witch who was killed for murdering her husband, who then came back from the dead and started killing people again? It's right out of a Stephen King novel. I know you like all that horror, occult, and all that other weird stuff, but it doesn't make it real, does it?"

Rylie looked at her with a disappointed expression on her face; she wished she had changed her mind about the holiday, the cemetery and everything surrounding it. No matter what Sarah said, Rylie knew in her gut it was real. Not only did she know that Mary and Edward Pascal were real people, she had that same strong gut feeling that Mary was a witch.

"Well, even if you don't like the holiday," she mumbled, "Can you at least hang out with me, Andy, and some of his friends? We're going to have a bonfire to commemorate but you can always sit back and make fun of the whole thing like usual."

"Let's not be so melodramatic, Rylie. Just because I don't think that people in the town got killed by a mass murdering ghost doesn't make me the bad guy here. Anyway, my family and I are going to Boston tomorrow after school to visit my aunt. We'll be there for two days."

"Oh," Rylie's eyes fell to the ground and her shoulders relaxed. "Have fun in Boston, I guess. It would've been fun to hang out with you even if you would've belittled the whole thing including the trip to the farm house. I told you I'm actually doing it this year, right? I'm going to make it into the Pascal house and I'm going to find out the whole truth."

Sarah laughed. "Okay, Rye, you do that . . . you be the first person to solve the mystery. You've never even made it past the drive before."

"I'm going to get Andy to go with me," she said, referring again to the farm hand that lived with them.

"Good luck with that."

Rylie furrowed her brow at her friend. Sometimes she wondered how they ended up best friends since the two of them were so different. The silence between them continued. Soon enough, she could see the brick building of the school looming beyond the town center. When they approached the school shortly after passing through the town, they trudged inside.

"I've got to go," Sarah said. "Student council meeting this morning"

Sarah hurried off to her locker and then into the student council room as Rylie made her way slowly down the hall. Her locker was not a place she enjoyed very much. It was right next to Brian White's locker; he was a basketball and baseball player whose clothes reeked for that very reason. Why he couldn't keep them in the locker room was beyond her.

She emptied the contents of her backpack into her locker including the two occult books that she had checked out from the library a few days ago. In the midst of her task, she was distracted by someone walking down the hall. Josh, the boy she had a crush on since the beginning of the year, was making his way toward his class. She watched how his brown hair fell into his blue eyes and how his shirt showed off his defined muscles. *Boy is he good looking*, she thought. He was also on her dad's basketball team, so she often made the excuse of seeing her father to catch a glance of Josh. He walked around the corner and out of sight, and she sighed deeply.

She took the books that she needed for her first periods. Just as she was closing her locker, Brian came up to her. She winced. Sometimes she wished that he would leave her alone and call her a freak behind her back like all the rest of his clique mostly likely did.

"What's up, Rye?" he said, holding his hand out, expecting a high five.

She just looked at him, and then reluctantly responded by slapping his hand lightly. He stood there waiting for her answer.

"Nothing much, what about you?" She was trying to be nice, but it wasn't easy.

"Nothing. But hey," he began, slapping her arm playfully, "You're into the whole Bloody Friday thing, right?"

"Well, as into a real horror story as I can be, I guess," she agreed, beginning her walk down the hall.

"Uh huh. . . ." he raised his eyebrows, but then continued. "Some of the other guys and I are going down to the Pascal house tomorrow. And we were wondering if you would like to join us."

"I don't know…"

11

He put his arm around her and pulled her close to his side.

"Come on, it'll be fun. Pitch black, haunted house, scary ghost killing people. It's right up your alley."

"And how do you know what my 'alley' is?"

"I know you're into Edgar Allen Poe, magic, and that horror crap."

"How exactly would you know this?" she asked, wondering if he was stalking her.

"Well you carry around those horror novels and witchy books. And I'm pretty sure that's all you ever talk about with that friend of yours."

He saved himself right there, because she realized she did talk about that kind of stuff a lot with Sarah, even though Sarah did nothing but roll her eyes at the subject.

"I guess you're right."

"Of course," he said, taking his arm off her shoulder. "So what do you say? You up for it?"

"I'd like too. But. . . ." She was having reservations about going out with a bunch of guys she barely knew, especially of the popular crowd. How did she know this wasn't some practical joke to play on the school coach's daughter?

"Listen, I'll tell the guys that there's a hands-off policy, if that's what you're afraid of."

Her hesitation was still strong; she really wanted to do this. But she didn't want to go with Brian; she wanted to go with Andy. Still, the urge to get into that house was strong, even though she was terrified at the same time.

She had a way a bottling up her fears and not letting anyone know, herself included. Frankly there were a lot of things that scared her, not just the cemetery or the thought of journeying into the Pascal house. She tried the best she could to not let too many people know those fears. She went on living her normal life but meanwhile she was scared of a lot of things: her dad getting over-worked, her older brother leaving, and the general impending doom of Bloody Friday. The bell rang, startling her out of her stupor.

"Can I get back to you?" she asked as she headed for her classroom.

"Sure, just let me know at lunch or after school."

"Okay," she added, and the two parted ways.

Rylie walked into the science lab and the usual coldness from the metal instruments and stone tables hit her. She shivered bit and took her normal seat in the back of the classroom. Most of the time she could be found sitting by herself and was only graced by the presence of another student if they had to partner up. Chemistry was not her thing which is why she always settled into the back and remained quiet.

After the rest of the kids filed in, chatting amongst themselves, the teacher started to drone on about some chemical reactions. Rylie felt her mind slip into another land while the lecture went on and only returned when they had to split up into groups. There were a few girls in the class that she was friendly with but of course today a group of the popular girls sat at her table. Rylie chose to remain quiet as they went on about the prom that had happened last week. Rylie hadn't bothered to go.

"Did you see her dress?" their leader ran her manicured nails through her shiny black hair.

"I couldn't believe that she had the nerve to wear that," the blonde, Courtney, chimed in, not looking up from the chemical that she was pouring slowly into the beaker, "I mean it was pretty much the same exact one as yours minus a slight color difference."

13

"It looked better on you though, Liz…" the third, another blonde whose name escaped Rylie, "You've got the body to pull it off more so than she did."

Rylie had to stop herself from rolling her eyes at the absurdity of this conversation. She instead just started to fill out the lab report not wanting to disturb the queen bees in their conversation.

"Rylie, we didn't see you at the prom…" Liz said.

It took her a second to realize that they were talking to her, "Oh, yeah I figured it's only my junior year I'll go next year…"

"It was so much fun you should've come," Courtney said with a genuine smile.

"Not really my thing," Rylie finished jotting down the rest of the report and then handed it to Liz, "I think I covered all the observations, but I suck at chemistry so you should look over it…"

"Looks good to me," Liz read through it quickly, "You have such nice handwriting, and mine is such a mess."

"Thanks…" Rylie raised her eyebrow; she had no clue why they were being so nice to her.

"You're going to prom next year right?" Courtney asked, "I bet one of the basketball players would ask you. We've seen how some of them look at you."

It was as if Courtney was speaking a foreign language, "I'm sorry… what are you talking about?"

"You know like Brian or Josh… we see the way they notice you when you're around your Dad at the game or practices," Liz added.

This was news to her but instead of turning into a giddy little school girl at the idea she decided to shrug it off. She wasn't sure if this was another way for them to poke fun at her. Part of her wondered if she would find a fake love note in her locker courtesy of the queen bees. Of course this was just a way to get under her skin; she was the freak after all.

"Oh guess I hadn't noticed," she then went back into her day dreaming as the queen bees, without skipping a beat, went back into their gossip.

They buzzed in her ear as her mind drifted into that other world it liked to visit sometimes. Their chemistry lab was done so it wasn't as if she really had to pay attention. Not ten minutes later the bell was ringing and all the classes were filing out into the sea that was the Summer's Hollow High hallway. She was once again another fish in that vast sea, swimming along to her next classes still in that sleepy fog.

By the time lunch came around, she was so tired that she found her head nodding onto the plastic cafeteria table. This continued until she turned to who she thought was one of her friends sitting down in the empty seat next to her. Instead it was Brian who still held that stupid grin on his face.

"Have you thought about the offer?" he grinned widely.

"What?" she asked not realizing what he was talking about.

"The Pascal house…" he said slowly the grin fading.

"Oh no, sorry. I've been in a hazy mood all day," she rubbed her head with the sleeve of her green shirt.

"Been there," he said. "Well, do you have any idea?"

"It's still a *maybe*. I was planning on going with my friend Andy. I try to go every year."

"He can come too, the more the merrier. What do you mean by try?"

"Have you ever seen the house?"

"Well one day I drove by, when I was going to pick someone up, but I didn't get a good look at it. Why?"

"It's creepy. It sends chills down your spine in the daytime. Think of how it would be at night," she said, not knowing why she was being so nice to him and vice versa, "Last year I got as far as the drive, when I could have sworn that I saw something in the window; then I just bolted."

"Maybe since a bunch of guys are going this time, you won't be that scared, and there might be someone willing to hold your hand."

"I'll ask Andy and get back to you, okay?" She prayed that Andy would hate the idea. She also wondered what Brian meant by there might be someone there to hold her hand. Was he the one that was going to be doing the hand holding?

"Okay then, here's my number." He took out a pen and paper, wrote it down, and handed it to her.

When he left, she twirled the paper around in her hand absentmindedly as Sarah and some of her other friends sat down.

"Why were you talking to Brian? I thought you didn't like him," Sarah probed.

"Yeah," Rylie mumbled, still fooling with the paper.

"You don't like him now do you? I mean it's been obvious that he likes you and let's face it he is hot."

16

Rylie didn't answer, but continued twirling the paper.

"So do you like him or what?"

"Who?" she asked, coming out of her daydream.

"Brian."

"Brian? Of course not!" she was a little too loud; everyone at the next table gave her a funny look.

Her friends seemed taken aback, as though they thought she was mad, and maybe she was. Was she really considering going with Brian and his friends? He might be right—it could be safer with all those basketball players. She had always believed in safety in numbers. Still there was something in the back of her head that thought maybe this was another "pick on the school freak" moment. As if they would go all *Carrie* on her when they arrived at the house and pigs blood would cover her once she walked into the house.

17

Chapter 2 – The Calm

By the time school was over, the storm had started and it was pouring rain. She thought about how much creepier the cemetery would be during the storm. These thoughts swam through her head as she quickly started out of the building towards the town center.

The rain came down in sheets around her. Thunder echoed and seemed to shake the buildings. She jumped at the first strike of lightning, and within seconds she was soaked from head to toe. Something in her felt uneasy so she stopped in the ice cream parlor to dry off and maybe wait out the storm.

She wasn't the only one to think of the ice cream parlor. Many of her fellow students had sought shelter there as well. Despite the crowd, she went in anyway. She shook her long-sleeved green T-shirt and jeans off, squeezed out her soaked braids, and found Sarah at a nearby booth.

"Some storm isn't it?" she said over the noise of all the people and the thunder.

"Yeah," Sarah agreed.

They sat in silence for a while, avoiding each other's eyes. There were times Rylie wondered if Sarah believed she was too good to hang out with her. It was as if Rylie was a little child in Sarah's eyes that she patted on the head every once in a while. This awkward silence continued until someone appeared next to Rylie. She looked up and was surprised to find Josh, looking just as good as ever, standing beside her. She smiled sheepishly at him and he smiled back.

"Mind if I sit down?" he asked, motioning to the seat next to her.

"Sure," she said, a little too quickly and excitedly. That giddy school girl that she had tried to suppress earlier seemed to be making its presence known.

She scooted over. His dark brown hair was soaked, and the part that was falling into his eyes was dripping on the table. They all sat in silence once again until Sarah's boyfriend, Chris, arrived. He sat down next to Sarah and put his arm around her.

Rylie had always envied Sarah. She had a boyfriend and she seemed so much more established than Rylie. Sarah was perfect at everything. She was one of the smartest students, she participated in tons of extracurricular activities, and she had a great boyfriend that seemed to care deeply for her. Rylie had never had a boyfriend before, unless she counted Tommy Acres from the second grade. She had never had a *real* first kiss.

"Do you guys want anything to drink?" Josh asked, reaching into his pocket for his wallet.

"I'm good," Rylie said that nervousness coming back.

"My treat."

"I can't let you do that," she countered, getting red in the face.

"Yes, you can. It's just a soda," he laughed.

"Sure, thanks," she fooled with her left braid.

"No prob."

He got up and Chris followed, reaching for his wallet as well. Sarah gave Rylie a look across the table; the first one she had given her since they had arrived. It was the kind of look that girlfriends give each other when they know a boy likes them. It was that of a real friend and it made Rylie smile. Rylie turned, watched Josh, sighed deeply, and

19

wished so much that he would like her back. She wished they would be the perfect couple like Sarah and Chris. That was just a dream, though.

"So, does Josh like you now or something?" Sarah asked bluntly cocking her eyebrow.

"I don't know. I mean, he never disliked me, but he's never shown interest in me - other than being a friend. We talk in the halls and sometimes I give him my notes to read, but that's all. Though Brian did say something about somebody wanting to hold my hand tomorrow night…" *Maybe Brian wasn't talking about himself*, Rylie mused.

"Look at you, now you're on a date with him."

"I am not," she whispered. "Am I?" Rylie added nervously.

"Looks like it, he's buying you things, so he's showing interest in you."

"You think? But why would he like me? I'm not pretty or anything, I'm just average. You hear what the cheerleaders say. I'm just a *farm girl*."

"Last time I checked so was I," though of course her perfectly moisturized skin and clean nails said otherwise.

Rylie investigated her own nails with the paint chipping and the dirt still showing underneath from tending the stables, "But you're pretty and popular, unlike me."

"You're joking, right? Of course you're pretty. Why do you think they pick on you and not me in the first place?"

"Because I'm not popular like you and they say I'm a freak," she replied.

"You are a freak sometimes," Sarah joked. "But honestly, it's because you're competition to them, you're one of the prettiest *real* girls in school, not like those skinny sticks that wear their stupid little skirts and tight tops."

"Ha-ha. I know you want me to feel better, but that is just a lie," she started playing with her braids again

"No, it's not," Sarah retorted, growing frustrated. "Why do think a lot of guys hang around you?"

"I get along much easier with guys. They're all just friends."

"They hang around you because you're *hot*."

"Sarah, stop joking." She was getting irritated with her now.

"No, it's true. I'd kill for a body and hair like yours."

"A body like *mine*?"

"You're skinny, but healthy skinny. You have a big chest, and long gorgeous brown hair."

"I do not have that big of a chest!" Rylie said, glancing down at her breasts.

"You wear a C-cup, so don't talk."

Rylie was a bit stunned by what Sarah was saying. Earlier that day, she had been telling Rylie she was weird for liking the whole Bloody Friday thing and now she was telling her that all these girls were jealous of her. Rylie had always seen herself as just average, and didn't really care what anyone else thought. She was never hurt when the cheerleaders made fun of her; she knew it wasn't true. She never imagined they were jealous, if what Sarah said was in fact true. Then she was reminded of the conversation, or lack thereof, that she had with the queen bees during chemistry class. Was she just blind to all of this around her?

"I hope you like sprite." Josh set it in front of her, startling her back to reality, "I didn't think to actually ask you what kind you wanted."

21

"Happens to be my favorite, thanks," she said. Sarah gave her another one of those looks.

Chris returned and they all sat down to drink their sodas. The conversation drifted from basketball to the prom that everyone but her seemed to have attended. Every time Rylie started something about Bloody Friday, she felt a swift kick under the table from Sarah. The rain began to let up; they cleared off the table and headed outside. It was still misting a little, but the sun was casting a yellow glow on everything. A rainbow appeared overhead.

"Need a ride?" Josh asked her.

"No thanks. I'll walk." She started briskly down the street while Sarah and Chris climbed into Chris' truck.

"Hey Rylie, wait!" Josh called, and she stopped.

He jogged over and stared her in the eyes, pausing for a second before asking, "Did Brian talk to you about tomorrow?"

"Yeah, but I didn't give him a definite answer yet. Why do you ask?"

"It was my idea to invite you, because I know you like that stuff. Plus, I kind of. . . ." He started to turn red.

"Kind of what?" she asked, puzzled.

"I kind of like you," getting redder he started to ramble, "Look I'm sorry I haven't said anything sooner… I meant to ask you to the prom weeks ago but that boat has long sailed. Think of this as my way of making it up to you."

Words were stuck in her head; she was completely stunned. She had never seen Josh this shy before around anyone, let alone her. She was beginning to think that there was some truth to what Sarah and the girls in chemistry had said earlier; maybe she *was* appealing to guys.

"Well, I like you too," she said, more confident than usual. "And I'd love to go with you tomorrow. Don't worry about prom. It's not really my thing anyways. That night I was fine hanging out with my friend Andy by the bonfire."

"Okay, that's great. Are you sure I can't give you a ride home?"

"I wouldn't want you to go out of your way."

"It's not out of my way at all. I have to pick up something at the Clark farm and your house is out that way, right?"

"Yeah, it is, just before it," she smiled.

They walked over to his truck and he opened the passenger door for her. She commented that she could have opened it herself, but he made a clichéd crack about chivalry not being dead. He started the truck and turned down the road into the woods. As they drove down the darkening path, she glanced at him every so often to make sure he was still there, that it wasn't a dream.

It had stopped raining by the time they pulled in her driveway and the sun had completely come out. She stepped out of the truck and her feet sank into the soaked grass. He walked over to her, seemingly admiring her. He was three or four inches taller than her, so she had to look up to smile at him.

"How can I repay you for everything?" she asked softly.

"For what?"

"Well, the drink and then driving me home," Rylie explained.

"Rylie that was nothing."

23

"Then how about this. . . ."

She stood up on her toes and touched her lips to his warm, inviting lips. He kissed her back carefully, as she slowly moved the tip of her tongue along the inner edge of his mouth. Rylie found her fingers in his hair as he now slipped his tongue into her mouth, tracing the area just behind her teeth. Her heart pounded hard in her chest. So hard that she was afraid Josh would feel it against his. The shock set in; she had never kissed anyone in this way before. His one hand was now at the back of her neck, while the other was placed on the small of her back. The electric connection that she felt lingered even after their lips departed and they moved away from each other.

"I think that'll cover it," he said, reluctant to let go.

For a little while she just took a mental picture of him and that amazing smile; it was so inviting and warm. It made her want to kiss him again, but she heard a noise behind her. She turned around to see her brother Matt. He was scowling at them, his arms crossed.

"I'd better go, I've got a bunch of errands to run," Josh said rubbing the top of his head and moving towards his truck.

"Okay, I'll see you tomorrow then," she frowned.

"It's a date," there was that smile again.

"You take all of your dates to haunted houses?" she teased as he shut the door.

"Only the ones I really like," he told her, leaning out the open window.

"I feel extra lucky then." She laughed as he started the engine.

"You should," he said playfully, though he still acted uneasy. She could see her brother out of the corner of her eye. "I'd better get going before he kills me or something," Josh added in a whisper.

"Okay," she sighed. "Bye."

"Bye, Rylie."

He pulled off down the dirt road and she watched him until she could no longer see his truck. Now irritated, she made her way inside the barn to grab some hay to feed the horses. She threw her backpack on a stack of hay, and picked up another with the hook that was hanging inside the barn. She ignored Matt, who appeared behind her as she moved the haystacks. He followed her as she walked to the stables.

"Who was that guy who had his damn tongue down your throat?" He growled as she set the hay down in one of the horse stalls.

"Not that it's any of your business, but his name is Josh." She swapped the hook for a horse brush and began to brush Edgar.

"Are you going with him now or what?"

"I'm sorry, 'going with him?'" She laughed. "Are we in the 1950s?"

"Oh, shut up," he rolled his eyes at his sister. "Do you know him well, or is this some sort of booty call?"

"Really, 'booty call?' Where are you getting these phrases from? Also, what is this overprotective brother thing? It's not like you at all."

"Maybe I've changed," he said, kicking a clump of dirt. "I'm going to be keeping an eye on you and this Josh guy from now on."

"Okay, Matt you do that." She finished her task and went to get another bale of hay as Matt slumped off leaving her to tend to the stables alone.

Rylie clucked her tongue, shook her head, and walked back to the stables. The noise of the front door to the house slamming resounded around the front yard. Her annoyance then shifted to curiosity when something shiny caught her eye. She sat the bale of hay down in another stall and stepped back to where she had seen the object. Stooping down on her hands and knees, she ran her fingers through the dried-up hay and straw.

There was a flash of red and she brought up an odd looking ruby necklace. She held it up to the sunlight to find that it had something in it. It appeared to be dirt, or dust of some kind. She stood back up, brushed the knees of her pants off, and inspected the necklace. By the looks of it, it seemed to be some kind of amulet.

With care she wiped off the dirty film that sat on the surface of the gorgeous amulet. There was something about this piece of jewelry that felt different than any she had ever touched. It was as if some kind of energy was coming off of it. It almost buzzed in her hand. Footsteps on the hay littered stable floor caused her to look up from the amulet in her hand. She was expecting to see Matt coming back but instead it was Andy. He then appeared by her side, carrying more hay for the horses.

"What's that?" he set down the bale of hay.

"Don't really know. I just found it lying in the hay," she held it up for him to see.

"Huh, wonder if it's worth anything." He took the amulet from her and inspected it by turning it over in his hand.

She shrugged, "I don't know, maybe..."

26

"Well besides finding this antique roadshow piece how was your day?" he handed the amulet back to her and started to finish moving the hay.

"It was okay..." she said slowly, "Normal class stuff and then ended up running into Josh at the ice cream parlor."

"Interesting. Josh... is he the one that plays basketball for your dad? The one that you always drool over when you go to the games?"

"I do not drool over him." She protested as she absently played with the necklace, "Anyways we hung out for a bit with Sarah and Chris then after he asked me out. Well, sort of asked me out anyways and then he insisted on taking me home."

He turned to her and half rolled his eyes, knowing very well how she acted around Josh. They walked back toward the house and sat on the swing on the front porch as the darkness grew around them. She stared intently into the stone on the locket.

"What was your brother so upset about? I saw him walking back to the house sulking," Andy asked. Rylie sighed and set the amulet back in her lap.

"Yeah," she didn't look at his eyes, "He sort of saw me making out with Josh and flipped out, though I don't know why. He never cared about me before; it was like we weren't even related. Now he wants to be all macho and overprotective."

"*Whoa,* back up there a second. You were kissing some guy you hardly even know? I can see why he got upset." Andy scowled, sporting the same expression that Matt had.

"Oh, come on, not you too. It's not like he's some random guy I pulled off the streets, Josh's from school and dad knows him from the basketball team."

It was her turn to scowl as she slumped back against the swing and twirled the amulet in her fingers. Andy continued to frown at her while Rylie just ignored this

27

overprotectiveness that both Matt and now Andy were showing. "So where did he ask you to? Parking up at the cliff?" Andy asked.

"Yes, because he's that ridiculously clichéd. No, tomorrow night we're going to the Pascal House to check it out, and it's not just us. Some of his friends are coming along too."

"I'm coming," Andy declared.

"You didn't let me finish. I was going to ask you to come," she said hotly. "But since you just invited yourself, you beat me to it."

Andy opened his mouth with a retort, but he didn't get a chance to say anything. A truck pulled up and the engine cut. It was Josh. Rylie quickly clasped the amulet around her neck and started toward him, a smile on her face. Andy watched in amusement, but he stayed on the swing.

"Don't get me wrong, I'm glad to see you, but why are you here?" Rylie asked arriving at his truck.

He held out a notebook that had her name on it. "I was driving back to my house when I realized it was on my seat. It must have fallen out of your bag."

"Thanks, I appreciate you coming back here just for that," she blushed and took the notebook from him. Her fingertips grazed his hand.

"Well, I also realized in my stupor after that amazing kiss I forgot to get your number," he chuckled.

"Oh! I'll write it down for you if you have a pen." She spoke with a confidence that surprised her; maybe today really was her lucky day.

"Sure," he said, handing her a pen.

28

She quickly ripped a piece of paper out of her notebook, scribbled down her number and handed it to him. "And now we're connected."

"Perfect," he said happily. "I have to go take care of some stuff, so once again, I'll see you tomorrow."

"Bye, Josh," she moved forward in an effort to kiss him again but apparently he wasn't reading her signals. He got back into his truck, started the engine, and disappeared down the driveway. Still, she stood transfixed for a while until Andy came up and waved his hand in front of her face.

"So. Josh, huh?" Andy's lips curled into a sneer.

"Yes." she rolled her eyes at the look on his face, walked back up to the house, and opened the screen door.

A draft blew through the house as she stepped inside. She trudged upstairs to her room and plopped down on her bed. Andy followed and sat down on her desk chair. Once again she fingered the amulet but could now see in more detail under the light inside. It had something engraved on the back that appeared to be written in a different language.

The words were engraved sloppily, as if whoever had done it had been in a hurry. She could barely make out the words: *Dormis es. Non Dormis nunca es.* She read them out loud, and it made Andy jump.

"What's that? It sounds like Latin."

"It's engraved on the back of the amulet that I found in the barn," she explained, taking it off and showing it to him.

He took the amulet and carefully inspected it. He repeated the words once more and sat there trying to figure out what it meant. Rylie remembered that he had taken Latin back in middle school before he started distance learning from their farm. He recited it once more to get the pronunciation right, and something curious happened.

A breeze swept through the room, even though the windows were shut. The temperature dropped drastically and goose bumps covered Rylie's arms. Rylie grabbed her arms for warmth and looked at Andy in surprise; she could even see her breath in front of her.

The chill subsided and was replaced by a rancid smell that made them both clamp their hands over their nose and mouth. Both of them were wide-eyed in terror. They sat perfectly still until the smell disappeared.

"What just happened here?" Andy asked, breaking the silence.

He glanced down at the amulet in his hand. He held it up to the light coming from the window and saw that the contents were gone. Rylie watched him carefully as he wracked his brain trying to remember what the words meant.

"*Asleep you are. Awake you now*," he gazed over at Rylie.

"I think we just awakened something evil," her heart pounded hard in her chest and she gulped.

* * *

That night both Rylie and Andy didn't sleep very well. They were both wondering what had really happened in that room. Both of them were terrified about what Rylie had said about awakening something evil, and wondered if it was true.

Rylie was convinced that Mary Pascal was somehow connected to the amulet. All of this was happening so fast. Her good luck had quickly turned sour.

Sleep just wasn't happening at this point so instead she hopped out of bed. She went into the living room to watch some TV. Andy wasn't in his room but rather already down there, watching cartoons.

"Couldn't sleep either?" he asked as she sat down next to him.

"Yeah, too many things running through my mind," she said not looking at him but instead at the TV in front of them.

Andy's eyes were on her and she could feel them while she was nervously twirling the amulet around her neck.

"What are you looking at?" she asked, irritated.

"Why are you wearing the amulet?"

"I think it's pretty, and besides, isn't it harmless now that the spirits are gone from it?" she continued to twirl it around her right pointer finger.

"Okay, I know you think that you're the expert on all things paranormal but it could still be dangerous, so why continue to wear it?"

She shrugged still facing the TV, "I can't explain it really, I just know I have to hold onto it." She didn't want to get into the energy that she felt from the item or the fact that she felt compelled to keep it close to her. Andy understood lots of things, but she wasn't sure he would understand that; she didn't want to risk sounding crazier than she already did.

"What's going on with you lately?" he asked sounding almost hurt.

"In case you haven't noticed, we . . . actually *you*, just recently released something by reciting that incantation or whatever it was. Maybe that's why I'm a little irritated at the moment," she retorted sarcastically.

31

"That's not what I mean. Ever since this thing earlier with Josh, you've been acting different, like you're so much better than me or something."

"Oh be quiet, I do not think I'm better than you. Nothing has changed except for the fact that I found out that for once not everyone thinks I'm a freak."

"Rye, I've lived here for what like 10 years now? Ever since my parents passed and your Dad let me continue to live here… and during all that time I've never thought you were a freak. Sure you have some strange hobbies but that is one part of you. Right now though it seems all these other parts of you are changing. When was the last time you were ever short with me?"

"Sorry… it's just like I said, Josh is finally showing interest in me. Then both you and Matt start giving him these side looks and acting like I'm some sort of slut for kissing a boy who I like."

She leaned back against the couch, hugging a pillow and sighing. Andy stared blankly at the cartoon on television. The coyote had tried to blow the roadrunner up, but had blown himself up instead. Rylie thought the entire thing was stupid; the coyote never died, even though he kept getting blown up and falling off cliffs.

Andy reached for the remote as the awkward silence continued. Rylie still sat there hugging the pillow, looking at Andy every so often. She thought about how close she was to him, and how he was like a brother to her. She did consider him family; she would do anything to protect him.

Andy didn't go to school with her. He did distance learning online, so he could be at the farm all the time, to watch over things. It didn't matter to him, he hardly had any friends but he always voiced to Rylie that he didn't feel that he was missing anything.

"So what time are we going to the Pascal House tomorrow?" he sighed breaking the silence.

"I don't really know, but Josh, Brian, and their friends are going to pick us up," she was still irritated.

"Okay. Rylie," he said, turning toward her. She stared back. "Look, I'm sorry I snapped at you."

"I'm sorry I was cold to you."

They left it at that, sitting in silence once more until Rylie fell asleep. She slid down the back of the couch and into Andy's lap. The dreams that followed were full of darkness and blood. She couldn't help but imagine what was to come.

Chapter 3- The Storm

Rylie woke up the next morning to find her head in Andy's lap. She noticed she had drooled a little on his leg, and wiped her mouth quickly. She sat up looking at Andy who was smiling at her.

"Sleep well?" he laughed.

"What do you think?" she asked sarcastically. "What time is it?"

Andy groped for his watch on the coffee table. "It's six forty-five."

"Oh crap!" she exclaimed, jumping up from the couch. "I'm late, I'm really late."

She ran up the steps, taking them two at a time as Andy sat on the couch, waiting for her return to the living room. Upstairs, Rylie rummaged around in her dresser and quickly withdrew a maroon shirt and a black skirt. She threw her shirt off, and quickly put on her underclothes and shirt. She slid off her pajama pants and pulled her skirt up while hopping over to the closet to get her black boots.

Once she was back downstairs, she grabbed her book bag. She was on her way out the door when Andy stopped her. "I can drive you, I have to go into town to make a delivery to your Dad's store anyway," he said, grabbing his keys from the coffee table.

"Fine then, but the truck better be loaded up already because I don't have time to wait."

"Yep, did it yesterday," he replied. "Let's roll."

He followed her as she reached the unlocked truck first. She hopped in, he started it, and they took off down the dirt road. As they drove down the road she turned to the cemetery behind her and her heart shot up to her throat. She swore she saw something or someone in it. She couldn't really make out what it was, but it was a black mass. The hair

34

on her arms stood up as she thought about what it could be. To calm herself down and push her heart out of her throat, she told herself that it was some kind of animal. Her hands shook a bit as she rolled down the window of the truck to get some air.

The trees swayed in the warm May breeze, but the air seemed rather stale. It was thick, almost palpable. It created an eerie effect on the countryside, but things grew stranger when they drove into town.

Andy pulled the truck onto the main road. There were hardly any cars moving around the normally busy intersections. That was very unusual, especially at this time of morning. Up ahead she could see the roof of the school. There was some sort of commotion up at the front. A crowd of people and cars were gathered around the entrance. Rylie didn't like the looks of it; her heart was back in her throat while she surveyed the scene ahead.

The truck swayed as they rounded the bend into the town center, and again as they made their way up the hill to the school. She could see more clearly now. Television station vans and numerous police cars were parked outside of the school.

Andy cut the ignition and they both climbed out. Police tape cut off the entrance to the school and officers stood outside. Some students were crying, leaning on the shoulders of the stronger ones; others had shocked looks on their faces. She saw Josh and his friends among the crowd and she went over to greet them.

Josh turned and saw her, Andy closely following. He greeted her with a kiss on the cheek, which she knew bothered Andy, even though she couldn't see his face. In the back of her mind she found this very public display of affection weird since they had only started going out. Then again, she was the one who had initiated their first kiss so maybe that's what he thought she wanted.

Her confusion about their relationship was pushed to the back burner by the scene in front of her "What happened, Josh?" her heart started to pound hard in her chest just like last night with the amulet.

"They found Mr. Akers dead in his office this morning," Josh explained, his face pale. "There was a knife right through his chest and everything; weirdest and probably the most exciting thing that's ever happened in this small town."

One of Josh's friends, a tall blonde named Alec, nodded his head in agreement. "Except for that time Old Billy O' Connelly accidentally shot his head off with his hunting rifle."

Josh and Alec laughed nervously. In fact all the students outside the school appeared to be nervous as well, looking all around or fidgeting where they stood. Many had already started leaving the area glancing cautiously within the crowd. There were a few teachers on the other side of the police tape talking amongst themselves, their faces pale and their eyes shifty.

Rylie felt uncomfortable asking, but she had to say something. "So, does this mean there's no school? Not that it matters, I guess, but. . . ."

"I'd say not, since it's a crime scene," Andy said, startling Rylie. "So why don't you come with me to the store?"

Josh made an annoyed sound at Andy's remark. He turned to Rylie, completely ignoring Andy. "You can stay with us if you want. We're going to go into town to hang out."

36

"Yeah, sure, I'd like that," she decided. Out of the corner of her eye, she saw Andy frowning in disapproval.

Andy mumbled a goodbye and left as Josh guided Rylie to his truck. She saw Chris and Sarah climb into the back of the pickup with Brian who turned his head looking at Rylie. Another boy, Rylie thought his name was Luke, was also in the back seat staring off into space as if lost in thought.

Rylie hopped in the middle of the front seat and Alec sat next to her. Josh started the engine and they took off down the road into town. Alec switched on the radio, mumbling something about not liking silence. Bad Moon Rising was playing and Rylie couldn't help but notice the irony. Only a couple of minutes later, they pulled into the center of town.

Luke and Alec lead the way as they climbed out and walked down the road. Rylie noticed that Sarah still clung onto Chris's arm, and she wondered if Josh would expect the same of her. This whole dating thing was new to her and she didn't know how to act. Josh though didn't say anything, just put his hand across her shoulder, steering her down the street.

Her mind began to wander. She recalled finding the amulet, how the room had become icy when Andy had recited the words, the stench that had followed, and finally the crime scene at school. She knew instinctively that they were linked somehow, and figured it had to do with Bloody Friday and Mary Pascal.

"Is something wrong?" Josh asked, startling her. "You've been awfully quiet."

"Just thinking about the murder and all," she explained. "I'm okay, though."

They continued to walk down the street but Rylie stopped in her tracks as something caught her eye. The town museum loomed ahead, its gothic lettering reflecting the sunlight. She was feeling that same feeling that she felt with the amulet. The museum was somewhere she needed to go, though she couldn't explain it

"Do you think we could stop in there?" she asked, motioning to the museum. "I wanted to check something out."

"Sure, why not?" Josh shrugged as the others studied Rylie like she was crazy. They followed her and Josh in nonetheless.

The bell on the door jingled as each of them walked through it. They all gathered in the small lobby. It was a tiny room that was furnished with a bench and an old desk. The desk bore a leather bound book where visitors could sign the consistently short guest list.

They signed in and headed toward the back of the museum, which housed the Bloody Friday exhibit. It was a little room, filled with glass cases containing a bunch of miscellaneous artifacts belonging to the Pascals. A book rested on a pedestal by a window. The book was filled with accounts of the Pascals, and descriptions of all the many artifacts complete with a rough sketches.

Rylie leafed through the book, looking for anything that might help her figure out the links to the different events. She then jumped as she saw something that propelled her back to last night. There, staring back at her, was a sketch of a necklace that was exactly like her amulet; it too was red and had writing on the back. She found she was holding her breath as she read the description.

The Cadmae Amulet

Named for the craftsman that made it, this amulet is said to belong to Mary Pascal herself. It was originally used to ward off dark spirits and Mary was never seen without it around her neck. After her burial it went missing. It was later found near her grave after she allegedly rose and killed the people involved in her death.

It is believed that her mother-in-law cursed Mary by sealing her spirit into the amulet. This was done so she couldn't hurt anyone else. According to the legend, the only way to free her is to recite the inscription on the back three times. It was believed that if her spirit was ever released from the amulet that the killings would start all over again.

Rylie froze in horror, realizing how much trouble they had caused. She reread the page over and over, looking for a way to reverse what she could only assume she and Andy had done. There was little doubt in her mind they had released the spirit of Mary Pascal.

Josh walked over and placed a hand on her shoulder and she jumped. He gave her a look of confusion that then turned to worry when he realized how upset she was. He glanced over the passage as she waited with bated breath for him to finish.

"Don't worry, it's just a legend. We don't know how much of it is real."

"No, it's real, I know. I found it and then read the inscription." Rylie's voice trembled as she spoke. "After it was read the room got cold and smelled rancid. We released Mary's spirit, Andy and I. We didn't know what we were doing!" she added, nearly hysterical. "Mr. Akers is dead." She lowered her voice to a hoarse whisper. "What have I done?"

*   *   *

Rylie stared off into space most of the car ride home from the museum. After she freaked out over the amulet and gave everyone there more reason to think of her as a freak, Josh decided to take her home. She knew that even Josh was apprehensive about her sudden confession that she had let this seemingly evil spirit out of the amulet. As she thought about it more, it did sound crazy. Here she was this normal teenage girl and now she was spouting off about witches, spirits, and death? That definitely wasn't normal and by Josh's lack of words the whole ride back she knew he wasn't exactly jumping onto this bandwagon.

Soon he pulled into the driveway and cut the engine. They sat there for a bit longer in silence and she thought of something to say about this situation that would give him a reason to believe her. Part of her was shocked at herself for reacting the way that she did and was scared that Josh was going to write her off and never talk to her again. Eventually they both got out of the truck.

They meandered up the walk to the porch and through the front door. Rylie was pale, her hands shaking. She sat down at the kitchen table, remembering the dark shape she had seen in the graveyard. One side of her brain thought over and over, *what have I done?* The other side was trying to calm the rest of her into thinking that maybe she had misunderstood it all and that this wasn't happening. She breathed in heavily and glanced about nervously, looking for comfort.

"So," Josh began, clearly still uncomfortable as he stood in the kitchen fumbling with a coffee mug that was sitting on the counter. "Do you want me to leave or stay, or what?"

"Stay," she said forcefully, her want for things to stay the same with him outweighing her bickering brain, "Want something to eat or drink?"

"No, I'm fine," he said as he sat down at the table.

Rylie busied herself by pouring a cup of iced tea. She fetched ice from the freezer and settled back in her chair. She sipped her tea slowly, once again trying to process all the events that had happened over the last day or so. This included not only the whole mess with the amulet but also with whatever this relationship was with Josh.

Josh still had that look of disbelief on his face but she could tell he was trying to understand or at least pretend to, "Want to tell me what happened last night one more time?"

He sat and listened as she recalled all the events that had happened yesterday. She told him where she had found the amulet, what had happened when Andy read it, and all the trouble she believed that she was in because of it.

With a start, she realized she was still wearing the amulet. She quickly withdrew it from beneath her shirt and practically shoved it into his hands. "This is it! The amulet! Do you see the inscription on the back and everything?"

"Yeah, I see it," he said calmly, turning it over in his hands. "But do you really think you let the spirit of Mary out? The smell and the cold could have just been a coincidence. But who really knows?"

Rylie glanced at him in disappointment. He still didn't believe her. She straightened in her chair, remembering that she wanted to talk to him about something else.

"I don't want you to get the wrong impression of me," she started in and he bore a look of even more confusion on his face.

"What do you mean?" he asked not sure what she was inferring.

"I'm not the kind of girl that . . . the kind that gets… physical so soon." Rylie felt her cheeks burning. "I mean, when we kissed. I just got caught in the moment, you know?"

He paused for a second as he now realized what she was talking about "I know you're not like that." His voice softened and he drew close to her, lifting her chin up with his fingers. "I was surprised when you kissed me. We can pretend it never happened if you want."

"I don't want to pretend it never happened, because it was my first kiss, and it was amazing," she said hurriedly. "Still, I hardly know you, and I'm not proud of doing that so . . . quickly."

"Let's just start over," Josh suggested and his tone of voice suggested he meant more than just the kiss. "You can have that first kiss again, with a guy you know a little bit better now."

Before she could reply, he leaned in and kissed her softly. This time it was a simple kiss only involving their lips and no wrestling of their tongue. It was sweet, warm, and the perfect one for the moment in their relationship. This one was much better than last time; it felt right.

He leaned back and his eyes twinkled as he gazed into hers. She smiled as she stared back at him; her brain seemed to stop bickering with itself for the time being and reveled in this moment with him. She liked him even more than she had when he was just this boy that she saw in school, at her father's basketball games, and crushed on. He was sweet, sensitive, and of course, pretty damn good-looking.

"You have the most beautiful eyes. They seem to sparkle when illuminated by the light," he said, transfixed.

She laughed at this mark of sensitivity and poetry, "Why, thank you, Mr. Shakespeare."

He opened his mouth to say something back but was interrupted by someone coughing behind Rylie. She whirled around to see Andy standing there, looking disgruntled. She glared at him but he didn't take the hint.

"Josh, this is Andy. I'm not sure if you've been introduced or not," Rylie said, gritting her teeth.

"We haven't officially," Andy said, outstretching his hand, which Josh shook.

Josh glanced curiously from Rylie to Andy. "You live here?"

"Yeah, I'm the help," Andy said sarcastically, arms crossed.

"Speaking of *help*," Rylie cut in rolling her eyes at his hostility, "I think Edgar and the other horses need to be fed, so if you wouldn't mind. . . ."

Andy scowled. His lips were poised, ready to say something, but seemed to think better of it. He went out the kitchen door, shutting it hard behind him as he left. Rylie turned back to Josh, an apologetic look on her face.

"Sorry about him, he's just a little overprotective, but he'll come around."

"That's okay. It's good to have lots of people looking out for you."

"Yeah, I guess, but when you're the only girl in the family, everyone seems to be on your case constantly. It's as if I can't take care of myself or something."

"Oh, that's right. Your mom left." Realizing that he had sounded completely insensitive, Josh continued, "I mean, sorry I . . . I didn't mean it like that."

"Don't worry about it. I don't even remember my mom," she sighed now a whole host of problems taking over her brain, "She left when I was four. Couldn't handle being in such a small town for too long. She wasn't right for my dad anyway, too high maintenance. She lives in Chicago, happily married to some rich guy, runs her own designing business, and pays no attention to us. She has her own family now, two bratty girls. And the only reason I know all this is because I read her biography in some magazine. Isn't that pathetic?"

Josh appeared shocked and didn't know what to say.

"We're better without her, even though our family is falling apart," Rylie said, though stopped as she realized she hadn't told anyone about this, not even Sarah.

"How so?"

"My brother, Matt, is threatening to leave at the end of this year and go off to some other state. He wants to do his own thing, in other words he wants to be free from work and responsibilities."

44

Josh's eyebrows furrowed and she could sense that he was starting to feel sorry for her. That was what she didn't want. She wanted him to like her for her, not because he pitied her or thought that she had some horrible life. Besides the crap that was going on in the town right now she was happy with her life.

"So what about you?" he switched the subject a bit. "Where do you see yourself in ten years?"

"I don't know. I guess I'll still be living here in Summer's Hollow, but I haven't really decided what I want to do with my life. I've considered becoming an archaeologist, and studying all about the different cultures of the world. But I know that's kind of stupid and it'll probably never happen."

"I wouldn't say that. If you really want to do it, then you should try to do it. I don't think it's stupid at all."

"Thanks," she smiled.

Their conversation had almost pulled her brain completely away from the murder and the amulet—almost, but not quite.

"About tonight," Josh began, "If you don't want to come, I'll understand."

"Oh no, I want to come more than ever. Maybe I'll find the answers I'm looking for about the amulet and the murder," her voice was a lot calmer now.

"Okay then," uncertainty still clouded his voice, "So what are we going to do in the mean time?"

"I was thinking of going horseback riding; it always helps. Do you want to come?" a ride was just what she needed to clear her mind before throwing it into the Pascal house with the rest of her body.

"Oh no, I don't do horses," he said, chuckling nervously.

"You're not scared, are you?"

"No, I don't know how to, that's all," he said defensively.

"It's easy, I'll show you." She took his hand and they walked out the back door to the stables.

She led him through the stable doors to Inkwell's stall. Inkwell was a Palomino, named for his unique spots, which resembled splotches of ink.

"Here," she said, pulling the stall door open. "You can ride Inkwell. He's nice and tame. He's kind of slow—perfect for a beginner."

She hoisted the saddle onto the horse's back and secured it. Josh appeared reluctant. She was about to go and get Edgar, but realized that she was still wearing her skirt, which was obviously not appropriate for riding.

"Hold up a second, I need to go change," she said. "You think you'll be okay out here by yourself?"

"I'm not so sure."

"Good," she ignored his statement and then took off to the house.

As she left, she saw Josh lean against the side of the stall, and looked around the stables. She hoped that he would start to like the environment more once he started to get used it. She still didn't want to leave him too long by himself in the stables so she ran up to her room and changed quickly into jeans. Before heading back down something caught her eye out of her window. Josh was in the back of the stables walking very slowly towards the woods.

That feeling of dread came back so she quickly turned on her heel and bolted down the stairs. Her stomach was bubbling as she caught up to Josh who was staring transfixed at something. She tapped him on the back and he jumped, whirling around to face her.

"What's wrong, where are you going?" she breathed heavily from running.

"There's something at the edge of the wood, heaps of something, lots of it. I was going down to check it out."

"Okay, I'll come with you," she said hesitantly.

They walked through the stables out to the field that sloped downhill. Rylie's stomach was creeping farther and farther into her throat. Something was definitely wrong. To her left was the fenced off area where the cows were kept, but they weren't there. In fact the fence looked like a truck or something had barreled through it.

Both Rylie and Josh clamped their hands over their noses. The edge of the wood smelled like rotten meat, and they quickly saw why. Lined up in a row on the edge of the wood were the cows, each with a stake of the fence through their bellies. Flies swarmed around them and maggots erupted from their sides.

As Rylie willed herself not to gag she counted that there were ten cows in all that lay dead at the edge of the wood. Josh's complexion was almost green as he stared at the carcasses with revolt. Soon the smell was too much for him; he ran back up the hill a bit and vomited all over the grass. She too could feel what little food that was in her stomach come up as she made her way up to check on Josh. She thought about how Andy had mentioned something about feeding the cows in the fenced area yesterday. This meant who or whatever did this, did so after Andy had read the inscription.

*　　*　　*

"I'm telling you, the three aren't connected," Andy insisted. Josh, Rylie, and Andy were sitting around the kitchen table, "And we should really call your Dad at the store about the cows."

"We have more important things to deal with than that, and I'm telling you they are," Rylie retorted. "Don't you think it's strange? First the spirit of Mary or whatever it is came out of the amulet, then Mr. Akers is dead, the cows are dead, and who knows what else happened."

"How can they be linked?" Josh asked as he slowly sipped water to calm his stomach.

"I agree with Josh on this one," Andy said, surprising Rylie.

"It's obviously Mary," Rylie snapped, her fear and reproach turning into anger at them for not believing her; "I think she's taking her wrath out on the town. It's because of what happened to her: the town murdering her. It's Bloody Friday all over again. She's a restless spirit that can't move on until her job is finished. You guys remember the stories. The years after Mary was killed, people would die on Bloody Friday. That was until the thirteenth year when her grave was dug up. Now that she's out of the amulet, she has all those years to make up for."

Rylie was interrupted by the phone ringing, and she jumped up to answer it. It was Sarah. She was talking too fast for Rylie to understand.

"Sarah, slow down, what's wrong?" she asked.

"Everything! First, on our farm, our crops are all dead, just like that and. . . ."

"*Whoa*! Wait I'm putting you on speaker phone. Say that again."

She turned on the speakerphone and set the receiver down.

"Our crops are dead. Mr. Nirton, the band teacher is dead. He was found in his bath tub, drowned, and the library is burning as we speak!"

They all had looks of terror plastered across their faces, as Sarah breathed heavily on the other line. Rylie thought how weird it was for Sarah to be this terrified. Usually, she was so calm and collected. The boys were dumbfounded, and Rylie was really sorry that she was right.

"*Now* do you think they're not connected?"

Chapter 4 – Things that were never there

That evening the six of them stood outside the Pascal house, each of them having second thoughts about going in. The windows were boarded up and almost all the shutters had fallen off. Even the barn behind it was decrepit; its paint chipping so it was more brown than red.

Behind the barn were the same woods that stretched behind Rylie's house. A mist clung to those woods, creating ghostly figures that seemed to dance about the trees. The trees themselves looked like phantasms as they swayed in the cool breeze that caused Rylie to shiver. Of course the impending task alone would've caused her to shiver.

They each took a deep breath and stepped forward; Brian was in the lead with a crowbar in hand. Rylie slid her hand into Josh's and they made their way up the walk to the porch. Brian stared up at the big oak doors that were boarded up; even that wood had started to rot away.

Rylie and the rest of them watched as he took the crowbar and pulled away the rotten wood from the rusted nails. He then turned the knob which was surprisingly easy though it made an awful squeaking sound. Brian hesitated before pushing the door open. He gulped loudly, the crowbar poised in his hand as if there were someone he wanted to strike on the other side of the door. He pushed the door open and it moaned loudly as it swung around, bringing the dusty foyer into view.

The rest of them slowly crept onto the porch and they all began to turn on their flashlights. The foyer was illuminated by six yellow beams. The floor was thick with dust and littered with the bones of ancient rats. Rylie held her breath, which she assumed the rest of them were doing, and stepped inside after Brian. Her grip on Josh's hand tightened and she glanced back at Andy scowling behind them.

After they stepped inside, Rylie expected the door to blow shut like in any typical horror flick but it just rocked slightly on its hinges. This unnerved Rylie even more as she shivered in fright and quickly closed it behind them. Josh whispered her name and she caught back up to the others. They made their way out of the foyer and into a hallway, which seemed to lead to the kitchen.

"We made it in," Josh whispered. "That's got to count for something, right?"

"Yeah, but now what?" Andy asked. "What are we looking for? Because I want to find it and get out."

"I second that," Alec whispered, "Honestly don't know why you all dragged me here just because Buffy here seems to think she let out some spirit on the town."

Josh shot Alec a look as if he had coached them before they came here not to say anything to Rylie. It was obvious that none of them, besides maybe Brian and Josh, actually wanted to be here. She just pushed passed them annoyed and walked down the hallway.

The house smelled strongly of mold and upholstery rot. Rylie tried not to breathe in the foul stench. They walked carefully around the first floor and soon reached the kitchen. An old-fashioned stove sat against the east wall, a basin for washing dishes against the north wall, and there was a large table in the middle.

The kitchen was littered with candle stumps. They were along the shelves, on the table, and on the counter tops. Rylie noticed a strange cabinet on the wall to the left. It was made out of wood, but glass covered the front of it. She shined her flashlight toward it and spotted glass jars and vials.

She let go of Josh's hand and walked over the cabinet. She gently opened it, for fear it would fall off the hinges. A cloud of dust erupted and she bent down, coughing violently. After the coughing had subsided, she peered into the cabinet.

A lot of the labeled jars seemed to be spices. Others appeared to hold the remains of salt, dirt, and strange items resembling animal bones. In the biggest jar, which was also the dustiest, there was a large black object that Rylie couldn't make out. The little vials seemed to be filled with the remnants of spices and upon looking closely she could make out some rotting paper labels on them.

"What'd ya find?" Andy asked, walking over to the cabinet.

"Some spices, bones, and assorted things which lends me to believe that she was in fact a witch after all."

"What no broomstick, no human hearts?" Luke chuckled but his arm still shook with reproach.

"Let's just move on," Rylie said annoyed once again that they all weren't taking this seriously and also that Luke obviously knew nothing about witches.

Rylie once again took Josh's hand as the six of them walked down the hallway to the foyer. They hesitantly started up the stairs, each step creaking beneath them. The creaks echoed off the walls and it sounded as though there were many more people in the house. Rylie prayed that they were the only ones in the house.

They reached the landing at the top of the stairs and a piece of rotting wood beneath Rylie's feet gave way. She stumbled into Andy who was in front of her. "You okay?" he asked.

"Yeah, just an old house gotta be more careful," she said, "Let's keep going."

There was a long hallway with doors on either side. Josh shone his flashlight down to the right and saw there were about four doors on each side. The left part of the hallway appeared the same.

"I say we all split up," Josh said, turning to the others as he apparently had taken charge of their expedition. "Rylie, Andy and I will go this way." He motioned to the left hall. "Luke, Alec, and Brian, you can go the other way. Okay?"

They all nodded their heads in agreement. They seemed too frightened to speak or argue. Josh was the only one who appeared confident. He made a good leader. Rylie felt herself glow with pride despite the situation. He squeezed her hand in reassurance and they each went their separate ways.

Rylie shone her flashlight onto the first door in the hallway. The wood was rotting, cobwebs hung in the corners, and the metal doorknob was rusted. They inched closer to the door and Rylie placed her cold hand on the rough doorknob. The rust scratched her as she carefully turned the knob and pushed the door open. A loud whine seemed to fill the house as it slowly opened.

Rylie let go of the knob as the door swung open the rest of the way. The room was painted an ugly orange-peach color, with a dusty border of what seemed to be roses. It was furnished with mahogany furniture: a writing desk, a bedside table, and a wardrobe.

There was a canopy bed with moth eaten peach curtains to match the walls and the sheets were a faded pink.

Josh stepped into the room in front of her and Andy followed. Rylie waited in the doorway. She had a feeling in the pit of her stomach that was growing into a certainty; she felt sure there was something in that room, something evil. She stared at the bed, unable to take her eyes away from it. Something pulled her towards it.

"Rye," Andy whispered, taking her attention away from the bed. "You coming?"

"Oh, yeah . . . sorry," she said softly.

She carefully stepped in, fearful that her presence was going to awaken something or someone. With every step, dust erupted from the area rug, leaving a film in the air which clouded the room. Andy went into the wardrobe, silently opening the big mahogany doors. There was nothing in it but the wooden back of the wardrobe and spiders crawling about the rack.

Josh shone his flashlight on the writing desk where a single piece of paper sat with a quill and inkwell. She watched out of the corner of her eye as he investigated the paper closer but nothing was written on it. Rylie then started staring at the wall next to the bed. It was plain, with the same color as the rest of the room, no pictures, and no marks. She turned away for a minute to look again at the bed. When she glanced back at the wall, she stifled a scream.

It was not plain anymore; there was a massive splatter of red which she knew was blood. Inside the blood was another substance, white, which looked horribly like human flesh. She stared at it, as Andy and Josh rushed to her side. They watched her as she stared at the wall. They saw nothing.

She tried to shut her eyes. She tried to turn away, but she couldn't. The bloodstain seemed to grow bigger, seemingly taking over the whole wall. It started to seep down the wall and collect at the baseboard. She stepped back. Andy and Josh both bore expressions full of horror, trying to see what she was seeing. Then Josh seized her by the shoulders and shook her.

She was awakened from her trance and stared wide-eyed at the wall, but there was nothing there. Josh stopped shaking her and Andy surveyed her, confused.

"What's wrong?" he asked. "What did you see?"

"I . . . I . . . s . . . saw." She stuttered. "Blood, lots of . . . lots . . . of blood."

"Rye, there's no blood," Josh said plainly.

"I saw blood," she said, looking up into Josh's eyes.

"Maybe. . . " Andy began.

"No!" she interrupted a little too loudly as she regained her composure. "I *know* what I saw!"

"Okay, okay. We believe you, just be quiet," Andy whispered.

"Let's get out of here," Josh decided, and the others nodded in agreement.

As they walked out, Rylie glanced over her shoulder at the writing desk. On the paper was written: *THE DATE DRAWS EVER CLOSE.* Her stomach leapt into her chest as she could've sworn that it was blank before. They left the room and Rylie looked at the wall one last time, saw nothing, and closed the door behind her.

Back in the hallway, Rylie released a breath she'd been holding. Then the beam of her flashlight pointed toward a door on the other end of the hall. It gave her the same ominous feel of the other room. The door led to the attic and seemed to be the key to everything. As much as she dreaded it, she knew she must go up there.

She headed toward the door, without motioning or giving the guys any warning. By the time they noticed her she was already there and ready to turn the knob. They almost ran to catch up with her. She stood there, standing at the door, just staring at it.

"This is it," she whispered. "All the answers, all the wondering, everything, is behind this door. I can feel it."

She reached out for the knob, caught it, and turned it slowly, slower than all the other doors she had opened in the house. The door opened to reveal a staircase that faded into darkness. Rylie took a deep breath. Josh took her hand and the three of them started up the stairs. Their flashlights bounced off the slanted walls as they climbed the stairs.

Each step seemed to last longer than the first. When they did reach the top, they all expected another step and stumbled onto the floor. They almost fell but caught themselves just in time. Thankfully the wood up here seemed to be mostly intact but they still proceeded with caution. They first took time to shine their flashlights around the room before moving at all. The attic was by far the dirtiest, dustiest, and foulest room in the house. There were many dusty trunks scattered around the space along with random mannequins, clothes, and chairs.

Josh took the first step toward the only open chest in the room and Rylie followed closely behind. Josh peered into the chest and blew on the dust-covered artifacts. Dust billowed from it and the two of them stepped back. They peered back down and saw books, more jars, vials, and a number of weird looking instruments.

One book stood out from the rest and Rylie bent down to pick it up. It was leather bound and burgundy. What mostly caught her eye were the raised gold letters that spelled out *Mary Pascal*. Rylie put her flashlight under her arm and tried to pry open the book. It was locked and there was no key with it.

The book seemed to be a journal of some kind; this was what she was looking for. The journal was why she was drawn to the attic in the first place. A wave of happiness washed over her. It felt unnatural, as if she wasn't really feeling it. It seemed almost far away.

It was then followed by wave of cold that swept over her that made her drop the journal and grab her shoulders. She was scarcely aware of the guys coming over to see if she was all right but she seemed to be drifting off to somewhere else. A sharp pain enveloped her abdomen that was followed by a cool sensation which knocked her over.

Everything went black and she shut her eyes. She felt as if she was dying and that it was all over. Sorrow and pain filled her head, infesting her. She dared to open her eyes. When she did, she was surprised to see a sunny sky above her.

Everything was different. She looked around her and saw that she was in the town square. Everyone was clad in long modest dresses with matching hats or full suits that were mostly faded. Rylie was then aware she was standing in the middle of them on some sort of pedestal.

She peered down at her bare feet, and then above her at the man holding the back of her green, tattered dress. It then hit her; she was reliving the memory of Mary's death. She looked around helplessly as everything seemed to happen in slow motion. Then she heard the crowd begin to chant.

"Kill the witch! Kill the witch! Kill her now! Kill the witch!" They yelled over and over and it seemed to echo in her mind.

She glanced once again at the man standing above her. He raised a knife up high in the air ready to strike. She tried to move, but found that her ankles and wrists were bound. She tried to scream, but no sound came out. The crowd started to laugh at her mockingly. She felt something hit her in the stomach, and she stared down at a limp head of lettuce. They then started pelting more rotten fruit at her.

The pieces struck her all over her body, covering her in an awful stench. The man calmed the crowd and they stopped the pelting. She was now covered in filthy, rotten food. She stared down at the pedestal watching her tears, Mary's tears, fall on the weathered wood.

She shut her eyes as the man yanked her head up. She awaited the force of the blow but it never came. She breathed a sigh of relief that then changed to anxiety. She wretched open her eyes and saw nothing but darkness. She felt soft, velvety material against her skin, but she didn't know what it was. Every part of her was in pain. Every breath in her lungs felt as though they were about to burst.

She craved air: cool, clean air. She reached above her, hoping to find it, but her hand struck something hard. Her predicament then became evident. She was in the ground, buried alive in a coffin. Screams left her mouth; she thrashed around and pounded on the lid.

She screamed until she could scream no more; her head and lungs felt like they were going to explode. She stopped screaming and began to breathe in, slowly cherishing her last breaths. Her heart pounded in her chest as she let out a blood-curdling scream.

She was jerked out of the memory and was aware that she was lying on her back on the floor of the attic. She sat up quickly and saw both Josh and Andy looking at her as if they had just seen a ghost. Rylie gaped at them as if asking for some explanation to what had just happened.

Neither spoke to her or asked her if she was all right. It was as if they too had felt the presence. Rylie wondered if they had heard what she was screaming out. Tears rolled down her cheeks and she felt like she was going to vomit. A minute later she leaned over and hurled all over the floor in front of her. Josh hesitantly put his arms around her and comforted her.

Andy just stared at her as if she was possessed. Rylie was so terrified that she forgot that they were still in the Pascal house. After she had calmed down, Josh helped her up. Andy followed them out of the attic, stepping carefully so as not to tread into the puddle of vomit.

Josh was supporting Rylie's weight as they ambled slowly down the stairs. Her head swam with thoughts and pain. So many emotions were racking her brain: terror, happiness, grief, pain, and sadness. There were too many different emotions at once. It was her guess that most of the emotions came straight from Mary and that somehow they were psychically connected.

The terror and grief came from Rylie. She didn't understand the source of the happiness. Was Mary laughing at the pain Rylie was going through? Did Mary enjoy watching others suffer?

Rylie became aware of her feet beneath her and her hand clasping the journal to her chest. A yell awakened her from her dreamlike state.

"Who was that?" Andy asked, pointing his flashlight down the main staircase.

"Sounded like Alec or Luke, or maybe both," Josh said, pulling his arm from behind Rylie's back and racing toward the stairs.

Andy and Rylie followed behind him. Rylie's sense of reality was back. Josh clambered down the stairs, a little louder than he should have. The yell sounded as though it came from the kitchen, so they turned left when they came to the bottom of the stairs.

They saw two shadows standing in the kitchen. Their shadows didn't move; they just stood there as if watching something on the floor. The three of them crept slowly toward the kitchen, not knowing what to expect. Finally, Rylie spotted Brian. His face was pale and eyes wide with fear. He was also splattered with what Rylie thought was blood. Alec was just as pale as Brian. Blood was smeared on his blue shirt in what looked suspiciously like handprints.

Then she saw Luke lying on the floor. His eyes were wide open, but empty. Rylie, Andy, and Josh rushed forward to Luke. He wasn't moving.

Rylie bent down with her flashlight tucked under her arm. She placed two of her fingers against his neck. It was strange how she had gone from being the victim, to being hysterical, to being the rational one.

"No pulse," she announced very calmly.

She inspected the body with her flashlight while everyone else stood there in silence. Once again she was amazed at her state; her personality seemed to shift totally. She had always imagined what it would be like if she came into contact with a dead body, but she never thought she'd be calm.

Luke had a knife sticking straight out of his abdomen almost perpendicular to the body. It seemed to just be a simple pocketknife, though it had done the job. Blood had seeped out of the wound and was splattered across his shirt. Rylie was careful not to touch the body anymore than she already had and leaned in closer to inspect the knife.

It was engraved with two initials on the handle: E.P. She knew right away whose knife it was: Edward Pascal, Mary's husband. Once again terrified, she jumped back from the body and fell onto the floor.

Andy bent down with his face as pale as the others, inspected the knife, and then turned to Rylie. He then quickly moved away from the body as the rest of them just stood there in shock. Rylie was breathing heavily and the scene around her really set in. Someone was now dead on the floor in front of them. Even though Rylie didn't know much about Luke, her chest hurt.

"Alec. . . ." Josh struggled to speak. "What exactly happened here?"

Alec just shook his head. His face turned pale green as if he was going to be sick. Brian just stared at the body, never taking his eyes off of it. It was as if he thought Luke was going to wake up. There was a brief silence where everyone just stared at either the ground or the body.

"So what do we do?" Rylie asked, quivering, "Do we report it to the police? It's not like we can explain what happened."

"No, we can't go to the police; they'll put us all in jail. And you just touched the knife. Your fingerprints are all over the murder weapon," Andy retorted. "What we need to do is dump the body somewhere without the murder weapon."

"He's not just a body!" Alec exclaimed. "He was my friend!"

61

Alec shoved Andy into the kitchen wall. Andy, who would never back down from a fight, shoved him right back. Alec fell onto the kitchen counter then got up and started back toward Andy. Josh squeezed in between both of them.

"Guys stop! This is not the time; we have enough problems on our hands. I think Andy's right. We need to dump the body someplace otherwise we could be implicated. We can't have that, not now, not with everything we saw tonight."

"So where do we dump him?" Alec said, still fuming, staring at Andy in disgust.

"I think we should dump him near the school," Rylie decided. "Then the police will think his death had something to do with what happened at school."

"Yeah, I think that's a good idea," Josh said his voice cracking. Everyone else nodded. "Now all we need is to find something to wrap… the body in."

They all took a second and looked around but saw nothing. Brian finally spoke up. "We saw an old tarp in the study upstairs. It would be good for . . . for this."

"That sounds good. You two. . . ." Josh said, motioning with a shaking arm to Alec and Brian. "Go get the tarp."

They both nodded then hurried out of the kitchen and toward the stairs. The three of them stood in the kitchen silently, listening to Alec and Brian's footsteps on the second floor. Josh opened his mouth and started to say something, but then he shut it again.

It was starting to rain outside; Rylie heard it pounding on the roof. A loud rumble of thunder made them all jump. It was then followed by a flash of lightning that lit up the whole kitchen. The lightning startled Rylie when she saw what it illuminated.

"What wrong, Rylie?"

"Look," she said, pointing to the kitchen wall.

There was another flash of lightning that lit up what she had seen. Written in blood on the wall were the words *REVENGE IS SWEET* in big scrawled letters. Josh and Andy both gasped when they saw it.

"You see it too, right? I'm not crazy?"

"No, you're not. I think you've been right all along," Josh swallowed hard.

"Come on, you really don't believe this stuff, do you?" Andy's arms and legs shook.

"Andy, I can't believe you!" Rylie exclaimed. "After all we saw tonight you still don't believe Mary is doing all this? You were there in the attic, you saw what happened to me, what she did."

"What exactly happened to you? You were screaming and flailing around."

"Not now. Here come Brian and Alec," Rylie interrupted.

Alec and Brian came running into the kitchen with a moldy black tarp. Each of the guys took a corner and laid it out on the floor. They went over to the body, but nobody seemed to want to touch it. Everyone just stared at it until Brian ran to the basin sink and vomited up the contents of his stomach.

"Come on, guys," Josh said to Alec and Andy. "On the count of three."

Each of them reluctantly took a part of the body. "One, two . . . three." They all heaved the body onto the tarp as Rylie gagged herself at the thought and turned away from the scene.

Josh took the tarp and folded in all the sides so that Luke's body was covered. Rylie just stood there watching them as they hoisted the wrapped up body and started towards the door. Rylie moved out of their way and then rushed out behind them. She was happy to get out of the house.

She opened the front door for them and held it as they carried the body out of the house. They started down the stairs and Rylie still held the door open. In her other hand was the diary and she continued to finger the circular indent on the lock.

As she glanced up the stairs once more, she saw a shadowy figure standing at the top of the steps. Lightning flashed, illuminating the foyer, and the shadow was gone. It appeared to be the shadow of a man.

"Rylie, come on," Josh said as the other guys got into the truck.

"Yeah, sorry. . . ." She shut the door behind her with her quivering arm.

A million more thoughts swam through her head as she walked over to the passenger side of the truck and got in next to Andy. She sat down and shut the door, not bothering to put on her seat belt. The rest of the contents in her stomach threatened to make an appearance. She glanced into the back of the truck and saw the tarp wrapped around the body. Rylie looked out the back window at the house as Josh started the truck and they pulled away.

It seemed like there was a light on in the attic, but when she glanced back again there was nothing. It was just her mind playing tricks on her. She had other things that she needed to focus on. At the top of that list was making sure that nobody would notice a bunch of kids driving around town in a pick-up truck with a dead body in the back.

Chapter 5 – Understanding and Denial

"Here's good," Josh said loudly, as he, Andy, Alec, and Brian set the body down with a sickening thud.

The woods were dark and coupled with the pouring rain they could barely see. The faint outline of the moon could be seen every once in a while but even that was blocked but the looming building of the school that towered up the hill from the woods. Rylie couldn't stop shaking as she watched the trees above her that were bending from the windy storm as if spying on their crime.

"Don't forget to take the tarp off of him," Brian advised.

"Why?" Alec asked, still shaky.

"Because our fingerprints are on it," he said.

"There's no time." Rylie shivered, holding her now rain-soaked jacket. "Let's just get out of here please."

"I second that," Brian said, also shivering his eyes still as wide as they were when they had found the two of them over the body.

It crossed her mind for a second that Alec or Brian might have killed Luke but she didn't say anything. Instead she joined in with the rest of their silence as they all walked back over to Josh's truck. One by one they all got in; Rylie sat in the middle between Josh and Andy, still fumbling with the diary in her hands. Alec and Brian sat in the back, both shaking. None of them said a word as the rain slowed, Josh turned on the truck, and started out of the school parking lot. He headed toward the town center, where there were no lights, besides the street lights, on passed midnight.

He drove straight through the town center and passed the library that was charred and barely still standing. The silence was deafening as he turned down 18th street and continued to drive until he reached a cul-de-sac where Alec lived. Josh pulled into the driveway and put the car in park. Alec quickly scrambled out of the truck, still white as a ghost.

"I'll walk the rest of the way from here, it's not that far," Brian mumbled, then scrambled out of the truck.

The three of them didn't have a chance to say anything as Brian shut the door to the truck hard and started off into the dark night. Josh just sighed, rubbing his face. Rylie placed a hand on his thigh; she could see etches of tears on his cheeks. He gathered himself and then backed out of the driveway and onto the street.

Andy was completely silent as Josh drove back down the street and turned back onto Main Street; he continued towards the west end of town. Rylie wrapped her arms around herself and gazed out the truck window at the town. She thought of how the town used to be so peaceful, until she had to be stupid and play with the amulet.

The diary felt heavy in her hands as the energy within it buzzed. It felt similar to the amulet when she had first discovered it. All that she couldn't find in the museum was in this book or at least she sure hoped so. Once she read the diary she felt she would have the knowledge she needed to stop whatever was happening to the town. The diary was the reason she was drawn into the attic, she was sure of that. The whole time she was in that house she felt like something was pulling her around and as helpful as it was it made her very uneasy.

The scenery changed as they entered the west end; the tree coverage became thicker and the road changed from paved to dirt. The water from her wet hair dripped onto Rylie's lap while she noticed Josh had his eyes fixed on the road. A look of both horror and anguish was on his face. They pulled up to the farm and all the lights were off except one: her father's bedroom light.

Rylie cringed. Through all that happened she forgot about what her father was going to do to her when she got home well after curfew. She was now aware of the clock on the dashboard as they pulled up the driveway; it read one in the morning. As Josh turned off the truck, the kitchen light clicked on, and the door opened. Rylie cringed again as her father walked out of the house. He looked both tired and angry.

Andy got out of the truck followed by Rylie, but Josh stayed for fear of her father. Mr. Bradford was Josh's basketball coach and because of this, he could have Josh benched. As much as Rylie wanted to talk to Josh alone, to hug him and comfort him after all that has happened she knew it was better to leave her father to talk to Josh. She walked toward the house but stayed in ear shot of them as her father walked up to the driver's seat of the truck where Josh quickly wiped the remaining tears from his face.

"Mr. Bradford," Josh said timidly. "I'm sorry we're so late, we. . . ."

"Now, Josh, you're a good kid," Mr. Bradford interrupted. "And you seem like the kind of kid who will treat my daughter right since it has been brought to my attention that you are interested in her. Though I have to say, when you bring her back at one o'clock in the morning, some questions arise."

"Sir, it's not what you think, we weren't. . . " Josh stammered.

"Weren't what?"

67

"Ummm we weren't doing anything. . . ."

"Illegal?"

"Yeah," even though that's not what Rylie thought he was going to say, "I can assure you that what we were doing was perfectly legal and that I didn't endanger Rylie in any way. . . plus we had the others with us including Andy."

"So what were you doing that took 'til one o'clock in the morning?"

"We went and saw a movie, and then my truck wouldn't start when we went to leave. I called Brian to bring jumper cables to jump start the car."

"Why don't I believe that?"

"Come on, Mr. Bradford, I played for you for three years now, would I lie to you? You can ask Brian or Alec, or anyone who went to the movies that night."

"Why didn't you call?"

"I don't have a cell phone. Then when Rylie thought to call you from the movie theatre phone, the theatre was closed."

"Nobody else had a cell phone?"

"No, sir, everyone else was gone, and neither Alec nor Brian has a cell phone."

"Either you're very good at making up stories, or you're telling the truth. Since like you said I've known you for a couple of years, I'll give you the benefit of the doubt."

"Thank you, sir." Josh gulped.

"Are you guys okay?" Mr. Bradford asked suspiciously now turning to see Rylie still standing a couple feet from the truck.

"Yeah, just everything that's been going on the past couple days has made me feel uneasy," Josh ran his hand through his damp hair.

"That's another reason that I don't want you kids out late. Seems that there might be a killer here in Summer's Hollow"

"You know, it could be something other than a killer." Rylie piped in walking closer to the truck.

"Rye now is not the time to bring up childhood horror stories… "

"If you'd. . . ."

"Rylie, why don't you go inside and get in the house, it's late. Josh you'd best be getting home. Your parents are probably worried."

"Yes, sir," Josh said and quickly turned on the truck and backed out of the driveway.

Rylie watched him pull out onto the road as the two of them went into the house. They walked into the kitchen where Andy was sitting at the table and stopped as Mr. Bradford sighed deeply. He glanced from Andy to Rylie and scowled.

"Are you sure you two are all right?" he asked skeptically.

"Yeah, we're just uneasy like Josh said," Rylie said, forcing a smile.

"About Josh…"

"What about him?" Rylie asked.

"Nothing, he's a nice young man and I know he'll treat you well, it's just. . . ."

"Dad, this is not the time to become overprotective," a shiver went down her spine.

"You'd better watch it young lady. I work very hard support you all and I've always been there to protect our family."

"But you've never actually been here for us. You're always working," she rolled her eyes.

69

"It's my job to provide . . . and you know what? I'm your father and I don't have to justify anything to you," he said raising his voice as his nostrils started to flare, "Now it's late so you two go upstairs and go to bed. Consider this conversation postponed until tomorrow."

"If you're around tomorrow," Rylie scowled and then trudged up the stairs. She heard her father say something else but she didn't care.

The stairs creaked while she and Andy walked up them, reminding her of the creaking staircase in the Pascal house. She hesitated before she stepped onto the landing at the top before starting down the hallway. Her mind flashbacked to the attic and she gripped the diary so hard that her hands were hurting. She turned to go into her bedroom. She stopped Andy right behind her.

"Are you really going to sleep?" Rylie asked, turning around.

"After all that's happened, I'll be lucky if I ever sleep again. That was some scary shit that we saw," Andy said running his hand over her face.

"I know what you mean. Look, we're on the same page when it comes to what happened, right?"

"What do you mean?"

"I mean you agree that all this is Mary. That..." she lowered her voice so her father couldn't overhear, "That she killed Luke?"

"Well I can honestly say I never believed in this stuff before. Now I can't *not* believe in it."

"Though you didn't believe me . . . at first."

"So you really think Mary is doing all this?"

"Who else would it be? Her house, her town, her legend."

"But still. . . ."

"Andy, listen to me," Rylie said, placing a hand on his arm. "With all the events that have happened since the night with the amulet it's too much of a coincidence. And though it scares and pains me to think about: we let out Mary's spirit. It means that I think we need to be the ones to put her right back where she came from. Something tells me that all the answers are in here." She tapped the diary. "If only I could open it."

"Well let me know when you open it. For now I'm going to go in my room and try to forget everything that's happened."

"Good luck. Luke's dead, and we dumped his body. The police are going to come and question us sometime," sarcasm was wafting out of her in spades since she had gotten back home.

"Well you know what? Until then I would like to pretend that everything's fine."

* * *

The next day the sun was shining brightly and the birds were chirping loudly. It was as if Mother Nature was mocking the group of friends in light of what had happened the night before. The police found Luke's body that morning and their preliminary report was that he had fallen victim to the alleged serial killer in the town. The people in the town were afraid to leave their houses but all the businesses were still open, including Rylie's father's store.

Her brother, whom she hadn't seen since two days ago, was nowhere to be found. There was talk that he was one of the victims, but Rylie knew that he had left for good. At least he wouldn't be there to get in Rylie's way.

Rylie sat down in a stable stall, leaned against the wooden wall, and fiddled with the lock on the diary. She tried as hard as she could to pry the book open but it stayed firmly shut. There had to be some way to open it.

It frustrated her that she was so close to finding the truth. She knew that the diary would allude to all the secrets about Mary, the house, the Pascals, and Mary's death. She already knew the truth about Mary's death and how the town had covered it up. It was an awful thing to bury someone alive, even if the suspect was a murderer or presumed to be. Rylie was rethinking whether Mary was a cold-blooded killer or not. Her mind went back to the very male figure she saw standing at the top of the stairs. It sent chills through her body thinking of him; she could find out about everything if she could just open the diary.

In frustration, Rylie threw the diary. As she threw it the corner got caught on the amulet and it painfully flew off her neck. She rubbed her neck as she reached over and picked up the diary with the amulet on top. Her fingers explored the cover again and realized something.

"Wow... how did I miss that?" She mumbled to herself.

Her fingers found the oval indentation on the book's lock and back to the oval amulet. She placed it into the indentation and pressed it down gently. There was a click and the diary snapped open revealing the first page written in cursive.

December the twelfth:

Edward and I have always had our differences but lately we have been fighting more often than not. I told him I thought that women should have a voice in society, but he just told me to shut my mouth and know my place. Edward hasn't reported me to the governor yet, but it will only be a matter of time before he does. We've been married for a year and a half now, but Edward has yet to find out my secret. I know that I should tell him. I shouldn't lie. If I do tell him, the first thing he'll do after slapping me across the face is report me to the governor. Edward has always been and always will be a man of law.

Rylie gasped. She had been right all along; she wasn't going crazy. Mary was hiding the fact that she was a witch. She'd thought it all along but now she held the proof in her hands. Rylie hooked the amulet around her neck, shut the diary, and stood up. Her long brown hair flowed behind her as she walked out of the stall in a hurry.

She quickly ambled out of the stable, across the grass, and over to her house. Her dad's truck was pulling up the drive as she reached the porch. He hopped out, walked to the back of the truck, and took a bunch of empty crates out of it. Rylie still hadn't spoken to him since last night; their silence continued as he walked toward the house and set the crates down.

Rylie watched her Dad walk back to the truck and grabbed some more crates. Andy came out of the house with bags of produce in his hands. He dumped the produce in two of the crates and loaded it onto the truck. She had no clue why they were loading more produce into the truck this late in the day. They always delivered the shipments in the morning.

"What's this for?" she asked. Andy walked back to the porch and sat down.

"There was a mad rush at the store today to get food. Probably due to the fact that everyone thinks there's a killer on the loose," he explained, wiping the sweat from his brow.

"Yeah, sure. How many people do you think know what actually is really going on. . . ." She stopped talking as her father moved closer.

"Rye, what did I say?" Mr. Bradford asked sternly. "We're dealing with a killer here, not some spirit or whatever other nonsense you're suggesting."

"Dad, you can't ignore the coincidence, yesterday was. . . ."

"Rylie, I don't want to hear you mention it again. It's just a story, so drop it."

"Fine," she said as he walked up the steps into the house. "I'll just talk about it when you're not around," she mumbled to herself.

"You know maybe I should take a page out of your dad's book and not talk about it either," Andy still crouched by the crates moving the produce around.

"What do you mean? You can't pretend last night didn't happen, it's not going to go away," her heart beat fast.

"Maybe I don't want to get mixed up in all this weird spirit stuff," Andy said, standing up.

"Why did you come if you didn't want to get mixed up in it?" anger started to rise.

"I went to make sure you were okay. I wasn't going to leave you alone with those guys."

"You've joined the club that doesn't trust me? You know this is a hell of a time for everyone to start caring about what's happening to me, especially when it comes to guys."

"Maybe because this is the first time you've actually been close to a guy that wasn't just a friend."

"You find it hard to believe that a guy would be interested in me?" she snapped, outraged.

"No, it's just you've never been 'that girl,' you know?"

"I really don't know. Who is 'that girl'?"

"The social butterfly… that gets all the guys to fall in love with her."

"Who says I want to be that girl? I don't! In fact I tend to shy away from the social scene," she laughed though still annoyed.

"I know, but you asked why we've started caring, even your idiot brother, and I gave you the answer. You're changing, Rylie. You're not the same little girl that would play tag with me in the back yard."

"I'm not a little girl anymore."

"I know, but I want you to know that I have *always* cared about you. I didn't start now."

She wondered what he meant by that

"I mean, you've always been like a sister when I needed a family. Your whole family has been good to me."

Rylie breathed a sigh of relief, looking at the ground. She was aware that she was tightly clinging to the diary once again. She glanced up at Andy, who noticed it was well.

75

"You got it open?" he saw that the latch was undone.

"Uh huh. Turns out that the amulet was the key to opening it. I should have guessed since Mary wore it around her neck all the time."

"Anything interesting in it?"

"I've only read the first entry, but it confirmed that she was a witch."

"Is that a good or bad thing?"

"It means I was right and now we know a little more about Mary. It's bad because it's apparent she's even more powerful."

"Want to read more and hopefully find a way to put her back in the amulet and get rid of her forever?"

"Thought you didn't want to deal with this 'weird spirit stuff'?" she said sarcastically as her father came out of the house.

"Andy, I'm going to need you to come in and help me at the store," her father said, carrying two crates full of produce.

"Okay. I guess I'll see you later, Rye," Andy said, helping her father with the crates.

"I'll let you know what I find out," she said lowering her voice as he bent down to pick up one of the crates.

Rylie watched them load the rest of the crates then walked up the stairs to the house and into the kitchen. She settled down in one of the wooden chairs and opened the diary in her lap. She turned to the second page and started to read.

December the thirty first,

I've requested a divorce for Edward and I but the governor denied it at once. He said it's not the puritan way. It is quite apparent though that I have to get out of this marriage soon, or I feel Edward will eventually kill me. He has become very violent. His mother, who lives in the house with us, always seems to look the other way. I have to do something fast before I end up like so many other helpless women. Helpless I am not, but Edward does not know this. For if I use magic on him to protect myself I'll end up being burned anyway. All I can do is hope I can find out how to get past both him and Judith, and hope that I don't have to take drastic measures.

Rylie wondered what these drastic measures were that Mary was talking about. Was she thinking about killing her husband? Was this the first stages of her plot? Was Edward's murder premeditated? She had so many questions she hoped would be answered as she read further. Rylie though couldn't help feeling sorry for Mary; she was just a battered woman, not a killer.

The phone rang and made her jump out of the wooden chair. She regained her composure and then picked it up as she heard her father's truck pulling away.

"Hello?"

"Rylie?" The voice on the other line sounded frantic.

"Yeah. . . ."

"It's Josh."

77

"Josh, what's wrong?"

"The police have already questioned me, Alec, and Brian. I don't think they'll come to you, but just in case I wanted to let you know what our story is."

"You sure are good at making up stories," Rylie said sadly.

"We said we went to the movies and then my truck broke down, like I told your dad. Then Alec and Brian helped us out. We never saw Luke at all. We had only talked to him that morning," there was sternness in his voice that masked his otherwise frightened attitude.

"So if the police come by that's what I should tell them?"

"When they tell you about Luke, act surprised like you have no idea what they are talking about."

"Okay," she agreed uncertainly.

"What's wrong?"

"I just have to get into the mindset that I'll be lying to the police..."

"Rylie, it's either lie to the police or risk ending up in jail. The police aren't going to believe us if we tell them what really happened."

"I know, I know…"

"I don't like it any more than you do and neither do Brian and Alec."

"How are they?"

"Still shaken up and haven't said much to me. Not sure if they blame me for dragging them there or not… At least the sheriff thinks that Luke's death was the work of a serial killer that has been terrorizing Summer's Hollow. Nobody seems to know what's going on."

"I think they do know what's going on; at least in the back of their minds they do. They just don't want to admit it. They'd rather blame it on something rational, which might be good for us. We can fix this quicker without people getting in the way."

"How are we going to fix this?"

"There was a spell that released her spirit, so there has to be a spell to replace it."

"How do you know?" Josh asked.

"Usually for every curse there's a counter-curse."

He sighed loudly and she grew worried that he was thinking she was a freak again, "And if there isn't?"

"Why are you being so pessimistic?" she asked starting to get defensive.

"I'm just saying there is a possibility that there isn't counter-curse or whatever you're talking about."

"I'll find one, don't worry. I just have this feeling there is one."

"How do you plan on finding it?"

"Oh, I didn't tell you?"

"Tell me what?" he was growing impatient with her.

"I got the diary open," Rylie was now annoyed with him.

"That's great, so you find out all you can about Mary."

"Josh, are you all right?"

"Yeah, fine. Ever since last night I've been a little paranoid. I keep hearing things. I know it's not Mary, but I just keep thinking I'm seeing things."

"I think it's just your imagination. You don't seem to be a likely target . . . no offense."

79

"None taken. But you—you could be a likely target after what happened up in the attic."

"Yeah, I think that was just Mary trying to get to me unless. . . ."

"Unless what?"

"I read the first couple pages of the diary and it confirmed she was a witch."

"I thought you already figured she was?"

"I did, but this confirms it. Anyways I've read before that witches sometimes have psychic powers. Maybe those powers could extend beyond the grave: all those things that I saw—the blood, the bed, and the writing."

"Rylie? What are you rambling about?"

"I think I might have a psychic connection with Mary. I think she's channeling me; she's trying to tell me something. Josh, I've got to go."

"Wait, Rylie I. . . ." He protested, but she hung up.

She slammed the phone down onto the receiver, took the diary, and ran up the stairs to her bedroom. Her bed creaked as she sat down and flipped through the book until she reached a page that caught her attention.

January the eleventh,

This morning Edward woke me in a rage. Judith found out my secret and revealed it to Edward. To my surprise, he didn't report me to the governor. Instead he revealed his own secret. He and Judith were also witches. They claimed to be more powerful than I was, with powers of telekinesis. They both made my psychic ability seem like child's play. Edward slapped me across the face; he threatened that if I ever defied him again he would kill me on the spot.

That's when I did it. He pushed me back against the bed and I opened the drawer in haste. I discreetly pulled out the knife we kept in the nightstand as he advanced on me and shoved me against the bedroom wall. As he reached to open my nightgown, I brought the knife up into his neck. As I did this he ripped my amulet off my neck; it was his way of saying I was not protected anymore. He fell back against the wall and slid down leaving a blood trail. It was on that spot that he died, never to bother me again, I hoped.

Rylie held her breath as she finished reading the entry. So she was right; Mary's power was a psychic ability and it was extending beyond the grave. This could explain why Rylie was able to see things that happened in Mary's past. She also remembered back to when she was in the bedroom at the Pascal house, and saw the blood and flesh on the wall. It made sense to her; Mary had wanted her to see it. Mary was using Rylie as a conduit to get her story out. Rylie was really beginning to question whether or not Mary was behind these recent killings or not.

Chapter 6 – Psychic Frequency

Rylie breathed heavily as she lay back on the bed. The diary was still in her lap and the amulet still around her neck. She knew that she had to continue reading to find out if Mary was behind the killings or not. Maybe it wasn't even Mary's spirit she had released from the amulet. What if it was Edward? He seemed to be a lot more capable of the killings. There was also the fact that the knife they had found in Luke bore Edward's initials. It was obvious to her that all the answers were in the diary.

She was scared; she was already so far into this that it frightened her to go any further. She took a deep breath and once again opened up the diary. As she turned to the next page, the doorbell rang. She sighed deeply and put the diary down on the bed. The doorbell rang again. She rolled her eyes and started to run down the stairs as the doorbell rang three more times.

"Hold on, I'm coming!"

She reached the landing and started toward the door. Then she stopped. Fear overtook her as she stared at the door for a bit, frightened of what might be on the other side. Her mind then settled as she unlocked both the dead bolt and the lock on the handle. The door slowly inched open and she let out a stifled cry of surprise as Matt stood there.

"What the hell are you doing here?"

"Well, hello to you too." He stepped inside.

Rylie closed the door behind him, gawking at him. She didn't understand why he was back; she thought that he had hightailed it out of Summer's Hollow two days ago. Now here he was standing in day old clothes with no luggage.

"Seriously, I thought you left? And why are you ringing the doorbell?" there were a bunch more questions

"I was trying to but then realized I left a bunch of stuff here including my keys. Plus there's some freaky shit going on in town. Everyone is on edge."

"Tell me about it."

"I can't believe there's a serial killer here."

"It's not a serial killer. There is a killer in Summer's Hollow, possibly two, but not your normal killer."

"If you mention the name Pascal I swear I'm going to strangle you."

"Matt, come on; it's the anniversary and the deaths. . . ."

"Rylie, it's a story. You take everything so damn literally. I told you that story when you were five to scare you. If I'd known twelve years later you'd still believe it. . . ."

"Matt, you know that the reason all these unexplained deaths are happening is not because of some serial killer on the loose."

"Rylie seriously, shut up with that shit!" he snapped, walking into the kitchen.

"Listen to me, I did something . . . something bad that let out the spirit of Mary, or Edward, I'm not sure who right now. Now they're killing people and it's partially my fault."

"Rylie, stop with this shit!" he yelled. "It's not real! Get that through that thick head of yours. It's a story that's all, just a fucking story! Get over it."

"It's not just a story," she insisted, "Did you hear what happened to Luke Masters?"

"Yeah, he was stabbed, so what? So were other people in town."

83

"We were with him when he was stabbed, in the Pascal house," she said, immediately sorry that she had mentioned it.

"What?" he roared, "Why were you with him? And in the Pascal house!"

"We were going there to find answers about what was going on and he was stabbed by something that no one saw."

"Did you actually *see* him get stabbed?"

"No, but Alec and Brian sort of saw him. . . ."

"Exactly what were you doing in the Pascal house and who was with you?"

"I told you, we were trying to confirm what happened back then and how it tied into what was going on now. And it was Josh, Alec, Luke, Brian, and Andy."

"You dragged Andy into this too? He's a good, normal kid. Why do you have to poison his mind?" Matt sat down at the kitchen table.

"I didn't poison anyone's mind. He was the one who wanted to go with me and the guys."

"Probably to make sure that Josh didn't put the moves on you." Matt laughed nervously.

"Look, Josh didn't put the 'moves on me' and he doesn't have the desire to." Rylie frowned.

"Oh, don't worry; he definitely has the desire to."

"Josh is a nice guy, even dad likes him. He's on dad's basketball team. Stop acting like he's going to jump my bones any second. You should just go back to not caring, that's what you're good at."

"You know what? Maybe I will. Not giving a damn about you worked out much better than what's going on right now."

"Maybe that's because you're a conceited ass-wipe!" Rylie exclaimed.

"Pulling out the big guns now, aren't we?" He laughed.

"Shut up and just leave. We don't want you here and I know that you don't want to be here either, so go!"

"Fine, I'll go stay with a friend but trust me, you'll want me back. Eventually you'll need me," he got up and grabbed his keys that were still hanging on the hook above the counter.

He walked out of the kitchen in a huff; Rylie followed him through the living room and towards the front door. Something made him pause as he opened the front door halfway. A look of concern flooded his face as he turned to look at Rylie who bore an expression of confusion back at him.

"Rylie," he said, trying to be calm. "I want you to know that even if it doesn't seem like I care about our family, partly because it's a complete mess, you'll always be my little sister and I'll always be your big brother. Remember that."

It seemed like a foreign language coming out of his mouth. He never said anything sincere unless it was accompanied by a sarcastic tone. She wondered if he was lying. This thought was pushed to the back of her brain as, all of a sudden, the door swung shut all by itself. It slammed so loud and hard that the whole house shook and Rylie's eyes widened in fear.

"What the hell was that?" Matt exclaimed as he took a step back.

"It was. . . ."

"Not anything supernatural!" he yelled, "It was the wind."

"Don't tell me that it was the wind; there's not even a breeze outside. Do you believe me now?"

"Rylie, there's no such things as ghosts." Matt turned around but was distracted by the sound of footsteps. They seemed to be coming up the front steps. The footsteps stopped and both Matt and Rylie held their breaths, waiting for something to happen next. The door burst open, admitting a bone chilling gust that caused Rylie's long hair to fly out behind her. She wrapped her arms around her body for warmth. Then everything stopped as quickly as it had started.

"You can't tell me that had nothing to do with the supernatural," Rylie said still shivering.

"I'm getting the hell out of here. I still don't believe it's the Pascals, but something freaky is going on here. I'm not sticking around to find out the end result. You're welcome to though."

He walked out the door, not bothering to shut it, ran to his car, and drove onto the main road. As she watched him, she felt as if someone was breathing down her neck. A chill coursed through her body as she turned around. No one was there. She shivered again and shut the door. There was definitely some sort of presence in this house. She hoped as long as she didn't acknowledge it, it wouldn't acknowledge her.

She took a deep breath then started up the stairs, listening intently for anything out of the ordinary. As she walked up the final step and was about to step onto the landing, the same sensation came over her that she felt in the attic at the Pascal house. She gripped the railing as the wave of cold came over her and she exhaled. Her breath hung in the air like it would on a cold winter morning. The chill was then accompanied by her head feeling like it was being ripped open. It was as if two people were fighting over it, each taking a lobe and tugging.

She fell to her knees on the landing and clutched her head. Her scream pierced through the house as she felt her brain about to be torn apart. Then all of the sudden the pain subsided. The silence in her ears became deafening and the coldness swept over her again. The hallway and steps faded and all she saw was darkness. She felt like she was plummeting head first into a pool of icy water.

Her body went rigid and she couldn't move a muscle. All she saw was darkness. She was swimming in it. She was then aware of every part of her body, as if she was suspended in a gelatinous substance. All at once she was overcome with the strongest feeling of vertigo. She feared that she was going to be sick like in the attic.

The darkness slowly grew lighter to illuminate a scene in her mind. At first all she saw was grass. As the picture became clearer, she saw she was in a graveyard. There were two gravestones next to each other; she was too far away to read what was written on them.

Mary, or whoever she was seeing this from, started to move closer to the gravestones. As she got closer, the gravestones became clearer. The first one read *Edward Pascal—loving son, lawyer, and husband*. Disgust overwhelmed her at the word *husband*.

The next gravestone appeared to be the same, except it bore a different legend. It read *Judith Pascal—loving mother and wife*. Rylie swore that she heard Mary scoff as she looked down into Mary's hands. In one hand there was a shovel and in the other hand was the amulet.

She drove the shovel first into Judith's grave and began to dig. Rylie couldn't figure out what Mary was doing. Rylie just stood there for what seemed like hours as Mary, with much difficulty, dug up Judith's grave. Rylie inhaled the putrid smell of death. Mary bent down and a casket came into view. Mary pried opened the casket and Rylie gasped as Judith's body was revealed.

Judith barely appeared dead at all, though she was very blue and smelled horrible. Confusion clouded Rylie's brain; she thought that Judith was the one who put Mary into the amulet, after Mary was dead. Rylie wondered when Judith died. If this scene was accurate, it couldn't have been that long after Edward.

Mary calmly reached into the pocket of her dress and pulled out a matchbox. She withdrew a single match, lit it, and dropped it into the casket. Judith's body erupted in flames, causing a warm glow to cast over the gloomy gravesite. After a while her body was reduced to a pile of ash. Mary stooped down after the flames had sunk into the ground and took a pinch of ashes from where Judith's heart had been.

Mary opened the amulet carefully, for there was already something in it. It then clicked in Rylie's brain that it was Edward's ashes. Mary closed the amulet back up and started to recite something in Latin; Rylie assumed that it was a curse. Mary took the piece of paper with Latin written on it and stuck it into a wooden box. Both the box and the paper were tossed into the casket shortly before Mary started to cover up the grave with the dirt that had once filled it.

Rylie realized that timeline might be wrong. If Judith and Edward were both dead before Mary died, and both cursed into the amulet, then who was killing all those people for thirteen years? It was now clear that Mary wasn't inherently violent; she had killed her husband in self-defense. There had to be someone or something else in the mix that no one knew about. She hoped that the diary would allude to who or what it was.

Mary finished and took a moment to wipe the soot and dirt off her dress. As Mary turned around she was met with five pistols. The police were standing there, one with rope in hand. From what Rylie could sense Mary didn't feel angry or sad or scared that she was going to die; she felt fulfilled.

Rylie felt like someone was pulling her back from the scene. The darkness started to overtake her again and the feeling of vertigo returned. It was as if she was ripping through time itself. She regained her balance as the hallway and the floor came back into view. Her eyes were unfocused and once again felt as though she was going to be sick.

She used the railing to clamber to her feet. She walked slowly into her bedroom and lay down onto the bed. The feeling of sickness subsided and her vision returned to normal. She opened the diary and began reading again.

January the twelfth,

I am now wanted for the murder of Edward and now Judith. Judith followed me after I killed Edward and we had a confrontation in the cemetery. As powerful as she claimed to be I was able to defend myself and she smashed her head onto the stone walkway. Now I am in hiding. I will not say where I am in case this diary falls into the wrong hands. Before she died though, she

89

cursed the town: mumbling something about as long as people believed in the supernatural they would still have power. I know I have to come out of hiding to curse them both into the pit of hell, or at least into my amulet. It was meant to protect, but when Edward ripped it from my neck it lost its powers. It will now become a vessel of evil, protecting the world from its inhabitants. I don't think it will stop the curse but for now will numb it. Because of my mission, this will be my last entry for the key has become corrupt. It is my hope that if they are let out this diary will be found and the truth will come out. In the event they are released it will mean the curse will continue with even more power.

Rylie knew this was the passage she was looking for; she finally understood the reason for the deaths. Mary hadn't cursed the town; it was Judith. Mary was not the evil that haunted this town; it was Judith and Edward. By letting them out, Rylie had broken Mary's curse and reasserted Judith's curse on the town. Rylie felt that there was still a part to this story that was missing; something had happened thirteen years after Mary's death to stop that curse. Rylie wondered if it had something to do with Judith's words before she died.

Shutting the diary, Rylie sighed deeply. The amulet now felt very heavy around her neck, as if it were dragging her down. It had lost all its beauty and she wished it gone. Now it seemed clear what she had to do. She had to dig up Judith's grave and get the box with the paper in it. Rylie was almost completely sure that the counter-curse was in that box and that once she had it she could send Judith and Edward back into the amulet forever. It occurred to her that someone must have dug up the amulet in the first place. Otherwise, how had it gotten into her barn?

She stood up and turned to her right. A scream left her lips as she saw what was written in blood on the wall. *THEY WILL NEVER FORGET OUR WRATH.* She panted and put her hands over her face, willing the blood to go away. When she opened her eyes again, the writing was gone. She walked over to the wall and it seemed untouched, unstained. They were playing with her mind.

Rylie walked out of her bedroom, shaking. She went into the bathroom and closed the door behind her, then gripped the sink with both hands. With her eyes closed, she turned on the water. She ran her fingers under it gently. All of the sudden the water felt weird, almost thick. Her eyes snapped open and stared in horror as thick, deep red blood gushed from the faucet. She let out a loud scream and jumped back. Blood dripped down her hands as she stared at them in terror.

She quickly ran forward and shut off the sink. The blood ran down the drain, but not staining the bowl. She grabbed a towel from the rack and wiped her hands off, but the tips stayed red. The towel fell from her hands and into the trash while she looked up at the mirror. Something out of the corner of her eyes moved; she turned around fast, but saw nothing. Her heart pounded in her chest.

Once again her hands shook as she turned back to the mirror and stared at the shower. That's when the shower curtain moved to the left. She gulped hard and slowly turned around to see if anyone or anything was there. The curtain was only moving in the mirror. Then it stopped.

91

Rylie stood perfectly still, too afraid to move; her eyes were locked on the mirror. The curtain was open two thirds of the way, but she couldn't see what was behind the other third. Her body told her to leave so she moved slowly toward the door. Her brain had another idea and she became overwhelmed with curiosity of what was behind the shower curtain. Her curiosity was exterminated as the curtain was ripped from the rings that attached it to the rod.

Without even a glance back she quickly opened the door and ran out of the bathroom. She ran down the hall and didn't stop until she had reached her room. Her room scared her now, but the bathroom scared her more. She locked the door and began to step away from it slowly as if she expected someone to come bursting thru at any moment.

Her breath was fast and erratic. Her heart was beating so hard in her chest that she thought it would burst through. She swallowed and sat down on the bed, gripping the covers. Above her she heard footsteps, which was impossible. The attic was all there was above her and there was no access to it except from the roof. She moved her head up cautiously and headed toward the door. Her eyes focused on the door, refusing to look up.

Something dripped on her head, but she kept walking. The drip continued and stopped her in her tracks. There was a faint buzzing noise in her ear, as if a bee was flying around her. She swallowed hard and slowly tilted her head up to look at the ceiling. A pool of blood had collected and was dripping onto the ground. She brought her hand up to her head and felt her hair. As she examined the blood on her fingers she saw that it was clumped and had skin over it.

92

She ran back to the bed, dodging the dripping blood, and picked up the diary. She ran to the door, unlocked it, and tried to turn the handle. It wouldn't turn. She let go and it started to turn by itself. The door shook violently.

The door stopped shaking and Rylie took hold of the doorknob. She turned it, and opened the door slowly, afraid what was on the other side. Once she was sure there was nothing there, she carefully stepped out onto the carpet. As she put her foot down, it sunk into the carpet. Water seeped out, making an audible squish.

She picked her foot back up and quickly glanced back at the ceiling where the blood was still dripping steadily. She gulped and stepped into the hallway. With every move, her feet sunk deep into the carpet and water seeped out. She made her way to the staircase, diary in hand, and then ran as she reached the stairs.

She jumped over the last three steps and hurried into the foyer. A noise that sounded like a dropping pot came from the kitchen, and then she heard it again. Against her better judgment she stopped at the walkway to the kitchen and peered around the corner. Pots and pans were flying everywhere and Rylie stifled a yell.

She ran to the front door and onto the porch. The site of Josh's truck driving up was a calming one. It was starting to get dark and it was growing colder by the second. She shivered and grabbed her arms. The chill in the air reminded her of the overwhelming cold sensation in the house.

Josh cut the engine and rushed out. Rylie ran over to him and threw her arms around him. Her whole body was shivering but at thing point she didn't know if it was from fright or cold. He put his jacket around her shoulders anyway just in case.

"Rylie," Josh said, rubbing her back as she clung to him. "What's wrong, what happened?"

"They're . . . they're after me," she exclaimed. "I can't go anywhere without seeing them. I found their secret and now they're after me!"

"But I thought it was only the Pascal house that you see things in?" Josh asked as he stepped back.

"I thought so too, but it's because Judith and Edward were the ones in the amulet, not Mary. Mary was the one who cursed them, not the other way around. It was Judith that cursed the town. They know I know their secret. Judith has tapped into the psychic connection that I have with Mary so she can freak me out! And you know what? It's working!"

Rylie gazed up toward the attic window. When she blinked and looked back, she let out a scream. At the window was a man dressed in a long black coat, yellowed linen shirt, and covered in what looked like blood.

"What, what is it?" Josh demanded as he tried to figure out what she was looking at.

"The . . . the attic, look at the attic. . . ." Her voice was barely a whisper.

Rylie watched him holding her breath, and Josh looked up at the attic window. The look of shock on his face was enough to show Rylie that he too saw the man standing there. Josh closed his eyes and opened them, and the started to back away.

"Let's . . . let's get out of here . . . now! We'll go to my house," Josh said frantically. As she looked back, a sinister smile spread across Edward's face.

94

Chapter 7 – Playing with Emotions

Rylie sat down on Josh's couch, still clutching the diary in her hand. Josh walked in with a cup of steaming coffee. She set down the diary and took the cup graciously. It was too hot to drink, so she blew on it and took a small sip. Her head swam as Josh settled himself next to her on the couch.

"Better now?" he asked, concerned.

"Yeah, a little," she said timidly, sipping her coffee.

"I know that everything has been really horrible for you. I know I've been scared to death through this whole ordeal. But we can handle it together; you don't have to be alone."

"But I am alone," she insisted, her voice shaking. "I'm the only one who can see this stuff. She's only targeting me."

"You're forgetting that I saw Edward in the window."

"That's because he manifested himself. Judith isn't making manifestations, she's making me see and hear really strange and disgusting things that shouldn't be there."

"Like what?"

"Blood gushing from the faucet, blood running down walls, dripping from my ceiling, footsteps in the attic, voices in my head. Then Edward throws things around and moves things, like my shower curtain and doorknobs. It's all too much for me."

"I'm here for you, don't worry."

She leaned up against him and he rubbed her shoulder in sympathy.

"I appreciate that, but you can't protect me. This is out of anyone's control," Rylie's bottom lip started to quiver. "It's a whole other world that we're dealing with. No one can protect me except Mary. But Mary is tied to the house; her spirit wasn't let out like Judith and Edward's."

"Let's see if I understand this." Josh let go of her and leaned forward. "Judith and Edward's spirits were released into the town, so they're free to roam around killing people. Mary's stuck in the house. . . ."

"And she won't be able to move on unless the reason she is sticking around in the first place is resolved."

"She probably wants justice to be served against Judith and Edward."

"Something like that," Rylie agreed as she took another sip from her coffee. "To stop Edward and Judith, we need to dig up Judith's grave to get the counter-curse. It's the only way to put them back into the amulet."

"How do we do that?"

"I think we have to be in the same room as them, or at least the same vicinity."

"So how do you get them into one place?"

"The best bet is to do it at their house, preferably in the room that they both died in, since spirits are usually tied to the scene of their death. If we get their attention, they'll come and then we can get them."

"And until then, what should we do?" he asked touching her thigh.

She was a little put off by this surprise gesture, "We watch our backs. By the way where are your parents? Shouldn't we keep the cuddling to a minimum in case they come home?"

"Some meeting in town, they'll be home late. You know it's weird how. . . ." He started to say something but then stopped.

Josh grabbed his head, almost in pain, and Rylie saw a shiver running up him. His face held a weird expression as if he were about to be sick. Rylie looked at him in concern. Just as suddenly as it had started, he was back to normal.

"You all right?" she asked.

"Yeah, I'm fine," he said. He smiled, a little too widely considering the predicament.

"What were you saying was weird?"

He had a puzzled expression on his face for a moment. "Oh, yes. It's weird being hunted by ghosts, having people around of us dying."

"It's not just weird, it's scary."

"That too." he cocked his head towards her.

"Josh, what's wrong?"

"Nothing. Why?"

"You're looking at me strangely," she said uneasily as she moved back from him a bit on the couch.

"I'm not looking at you strangely; I'm just *looking* at you." He wasn't blinking.

"Josh, you're creeping me out."

"You know . . . you look a lot like her," he said, brushing a loose strand of hair out of her face.

As soon as his hand touched the side of her face, she was overcome by coldness; his hands were icy. She recoiled, and he noticed it. Fear welled up inside her.

"Like . . . like who?" Rylie stammered, pushing his ice-cold hand out of her face.

"Mary," he replied, smiling. "You have the same eyes, and you both have the same body type." He stared at her as though he was trying to memorize every curve of her body.

"Josh, I think it's time for me to go."

"Stay," he implored her, grabbing her arm. Another wave of cold moved through her body.

"No, Josh, let me go!" she said, trying to get up.

Josh pushed her down, pinning her against the couch cushions. She tried to push him away but he was too strong. He bore down on her, kissing her neck with his frozen lips.

"Josh, get the hell off me!" she yelled, thrashing about beneath him.

Her body was rigid from cold; she could see her breath. He still kissed her neck, his face hidden from view.

"You scream like her, too." Josh laughed, but his voice sounded different, and deeper. He sounded smug.

He lifted his head up to look at her, and she saw that it wasn't Josh on top of her. She was staring right into the face of Edward Pascal. She let out a blood-curdling scream and tried to push him away. His clothes were ripped and bloody; his face was pale and had a bluish tint to it. His eyes seemed to sink into his face. The smell of decaying flesh and the grave permeated the air.

He continued to kiss her and attempted to pull up her shirt. She screamed aloud again and kicked him in the groin. He fell back onto the couch and she ran toward the front door. She grabbed the knob, but the door wouldn't budge. She tried harder but it still wouldn't turn. A cold hand clamped down on the back of her neck and she screamed again.

The knob was stuck in place; she shook it hard and started to cry in fright. The hand on the back of her neck grew tighter until Edward whirled her around to face him. He pushed her against the door and kept his hand around her neck. He started to crush her throat and she gasped for air.

"I'm not going to let you put us back," Edward said. His eerie voice sounded gravelly. "We're having too much fun with the old town, but boy has it changed. Have to thank you for releasing us in the first place. I had just enough power left to make sure it got into somebody's hands."

"You're not going to get away with this." Rylie gasped.

"I think I will. With you and your boyfriend dead no one else knows how to get rid of us. It's like old times again."

She couldn't talk now; he was smashing her trachea and she couldn't even gasp for air. He just smiled at her through rotten teeth. Rylie kicked him in the shin and he let go of her. She ran as fast as she could into the kitchen, shut the door behind her, and locked it fast.

She stepped back from it slowly, coughing, and holding her neck in pain. Her reflection in the toaster made her stop and she walked closer to it. There were marks on her neck where he tried to strangle her. Banging sounded at the door and startled her. She ran over to the counter and started to open drawers, looking for anything she could use to protect herself.

99

There was a drawer full of knives and she picked out a particularly big steak knife. She quickly closed the drawer and ran behind the counter in the middle of the kitchen. Then all of the sudden the lock broke on the door and it flew open. She crouched behind the counter and waited, listening, and trying to keep as quiet as possible.

The room went silent until she heard footsteps walking into the kitchen. There was a crash as he knocked something off of the counter; then there was silence again. All of the sudden the drawer full of knives was flying toward her; the knives pointed at her head. She ducked and ran over to the wall.

The wall acted as her support as she gripped the knife in her right hand down by her side. Edward advanced on her, making things fly all over the room. Two forks flew into the wall on either side of her and she sprinted toward the door and away from Edward. As she was about to go through the door, she felt herself being lifted off the ground and go sailing through the air. She landed with a hard thud against the living room wall.

Her head started to pound in pain and when she went up to feel it, blood covered her hand. She tried to move, but he wouldn't let her. He walked over to her, raising her up into the standing position. She raised the knife at him, but he forced it out of her hands and into his. He held her back against the wall with his powers so that she couldn't move a muscle. Every part of her body was being controlled.

"So this is it, the end of your life and shortly after the end of your boyfriend's life, your father's, your brother's, your friends' . . . Any last words?"

She couldn't move her mouth; he knew that and laughed horribly. As he was about to strike, a weird sensation came over her. Even though Edward was controlling her, her arm extended in front of her and her hand clenched into a fist.

Even Edward seemed surprised. Whoever was controlling her body now drove her fist into Edward's face with enough force to knock him over. The punch was powered by an extremely powerful force. Rylie had a strong feeling that it was Mary.

The knife was knocked out of Edward's hand. Rylie scooped it up immediately and lowered herself over Edward, the knife up against his neck. His eyes were closed, but he was still conscious. Something told her that his power emanated from his eyes. If his eyes were closed, she was safe.

The knife moved from his neck and pressed into his cheek. She dragged the knife down his cheek so that a cut was visible. Blood seeped from it, and he winced. His eyes snapped open to reveal a soulless black color. He lifted himself up eerily. Her eyes grew wide in fear.

His mouth opened wide to reveal nothingness and face twisted into a horrifying position. She tried to look away but he wouldn't let her. He brought her too him, gliding her across the floor, her toes barely scraping the carpet. The knife was still in her hand but once again he controlled every part of her body.

She prayed that Mary would control her body and her prayer was answered as her right hand lifted the knife up so the blade was facing Edward. Those eyes stared at the knife in both mockery and horror. Her arm was wrenched back, the blade still focused on Edward, and then she threw the knife with great force.

The knife went sailing through the air at an alarming rate and landed right in his eye. The black eye exploded with blood. It went everywhere, all over Rylie, covering her gray shirt. Edward's power on her was released and she fell hard to the floor, causing blood to drip out of her head wound.

She watched as Edward writhed in pain, pulled the knife out of his eye, and fell back onto the floor. He laid there, the bloody knife next to him, until she heard a high-pitched wailing. It was followed by a tremendous wind that went all around the living room, swung the door wide open, and ceased.

Breathing heavily, she sat up and crawled over to Edward's body. As she got closer, she saw that it wasn't his body, but Josh's. She let out a tiny cry and rushed over to him. His eye was still whole, but there was a cut across his cheek. He seemed conscious. She helped him to the sitting the position as blood dribbled from his wound.

"Oh, Josh," tears stung her eyes and blood dripped from her head. "Are you okay? I'm so sorry, you looked like him. He was you; I mean . . . I'm just so sorry."

She threw her arms around him as tears ran down her face. Josh patted her back in reassurance. Blood dripped from his cut and onto her already bloodstained shirt. Now was when she noticed that it was only her blood on her. Edward's blood was gone leading her to believe it was all just another illusion.

Josh let go of her and she helped him to his feet, "I'm so sorry, Rye," there was a look of remorse on his face. "I tried to stop him from hurting you, but he had total control over my body. I couldn't even breathe on my own. I'm so sorry he hurt you. I could see it all happening and couldn't do a thing."

"It's okay. I know it's not your fault. You didn't ask him to take over your body," but part of her was still apprehensive towards him. "And I'm sorry that I cut you."

"You were only trying to defend yourself," he said knowingly.

"We should try to stitch that up," she walked over to the kitchen.

"Rylie, I'm fine," he said, following her. "It's just a scratch. Your head, though. . . ."

102

"I'm fine; head wounds bleed a lot, that's all. I don't need anything but let me put something on your cheek," she insisted, rummaging through the medicine cabinet for something to help him.

"Rylie, why don't we figure out how to fix this ghost problem instead of you trying to. . . " He was cut off as Rylie put a dish towel with hydrogen peroxide she found in the cabinet on his cheek "Ow! That stings."

"Just relax," she said distantly as she continued to hold the towel to his face.

They walked back over to the couch and settled themselves on the cushions. She hesitated to touch him but then shook off that feeling and placed the towel against his cut again. He flinched and she sighed. Rylie pulled the towel away from Josh's face to examine the cut. Her arm was still shaking. The hydrogen peroxide was bubbling in the cut and the bleeding had stopped.

"Looks fine now. We just need a bandage," she said, about to stand up.

"No, no bandage."

"Okay, but be careful from now on," she said, placing the bloody towel on the coffee table.

"As long as you don't come at me with any more knives, I think I'll be fine," a smile passed his lips.

"Josh, I said I was sorry," tears welled up in her eyes.

"Rylie, I was kidding…" he realized that what he said was insensitive

"Don't joke like that, I feel bad enough about slicing my boyfriend," she turned away from him as tears fell down her face.

He sighed and pulled her towards him. At first she resisted but then gave in and let him hold her as she continued to cry. After a while Josh spoke up, "So do you think we should get to the graveyard and find that counter-curse or whatever?"

"That sounds like a good idea," her tears slowly stopped, "I guess we can go to my house… grab some tools, and dig up the grave."

"By the time we get there, it'll be dark," Josh said. Now he sounded uneasy.

"Yeah, that's the perfect time to do it so no one sees us," she stood up regaining her composure, "Desecrating holy ground is a crime; we could go to jail for it."

"Great, we can tack on grave robbing with murder and breaking and entering," he said sarcastically.

"Josh, if you don't want to go with me, I'll understand. It's a lot to handle; all the laws we've broken all the things that we've seen. If you quit now I won't think badly of you. I dragged you into this," her voice caught again, "I know you were the one who took me to the house, but I'm the one who started this whole mess. I'm the one who let out the spirits, me and Andy. But you're not a part of it; you don't have to help us."

"That's where you're mistaken; I became a part of this when Edward hijacked my body and tried to kill my girlfriend. I'm in this, Rylie. I know you don't want me to get hurt, but now it's personal."

*　　*　　*

Rylie and Josh stood in the stables with shovels in hand. In her other hand, Rylie held the diary; the amulet hung around her neck. By now it was ten o'clock and

104

completely dark outside. The house was empty since her father was still at the store, but she heard a truck pull up in the driveway.

Curiosity got the best of Rylie and she walked out of the stables with the shovel and diary still in hand. It was Andy; he was walking toward the house. He stopped in his tracks when he saw Rylie and Josh.

"What's with the shovels?" he asked walking towards them.

"Apparently we're going to dig up a grave," Josh looked apprehensively at the shovel.

"Oh great, something else we can add to our police record."

"What do you mean *we*?" Rylie asked.

"Like I'm going to let you guys go into the cemetery by yourselves in the middle of the night when psycho ghosts are after all of us."

"So is it the ghosts you're worried about?" Josh said, putting his shovel down against the porch. "Or is it me that you have a problem with?"

"Now that you mention it, it's both actually," Andy replied, walking over to Josh.

"Guys. . . ." Rylie said.

"I knew you had a problem with me. So what is it, the fact that I'm a jock or the fact that I'm going out with your friend?"

"Both," Andy said, putting his face up to Josh's. They were about the same height but Josh was a little taller than Andy. "Guys like you have a reputation."

"I'm not like most guys, I treat Rylie with respect. The reason I think you have a problem with me is because I'm going out with someone you secretly have feelings for."

"Hello, I'm right here," Rylie said, but they ignored her.

"Nice try, but no. I just don't like you; you and Rylie are not right for each other. Plus you just started dating like what . . . two days ago?"

"So?"

"So? Don't you think you're moving a little too fast?"

"I've known her for a while. Her father is my coach. We haven't even gotten that serious yet and I don't plan to get serious until we're both ready."

"Why Rylie, though? There are so many superficial cheerleaders for you to hook up with, why pick someone like her?"

"Hey!" Rylie exclaimed. "What is that supposed to mean?"

"You know what I mean," Andy rolled his eyes.

"I wanted to go out with her because she *wasn't* a superficial cheerleader. I was sick of dating girls like that. Then I met Rylie, who was prettier than them anyway." she blushed. "And she was so perfectly not perfect, and that's what I liked about her."

Andy tried to say more, but Rylie knew that he couldn't cut down Josh anymore. She thought he was realizing he wasn't the person that he had expected him to be.

"Can you seriously just stop with this? This isn't the time. People are dying and we need to fix it. We don't stupid teenage drama on top of it all, so please make up so that we can get back to business?" Rylie said, frustrated.

"Fine," Andy said. "You can date her for the time being. But if you hurt her, I'll kill you."

"Wouldn't expect any less," Josh said sarcastically.

"Now shake hands and let's get over to the cemetery," Rylie said impatiently.

106

They shook hands reluctantly and stepped away from each other. Josh picked up his shovel and slung it over his shoulder. The moon shone brightly as they stood on the lawn and Andy noticed that they were both covered in blood.

"What the hell happened to you two?" Andy asked as he glanced from the cut across Josh's cheek to the dried blood on the back of Rylie's head.

"Let's just say Edward paid us a little visit," Josh said, looking at the ground.

"Yeah, and he's not happy at all to say the least. He tried to kill me, and now he knows our plan."

"Where were you, Josh, when your girlfriend was being attacked by Edward?"

"I well... Edward used my body as a kind of. . . "

"Shell," Rylie finished, knowing Josh didn't know how to explain it. "He took over Josh's body and then tried to kill me. Then he used his powers on me and almost killed me if it hadn't been for Mary."

"Mary?" Andy asked.

"The psychic connection that I have with her must be getting stronger. She took over my body when Edward tried to control me."

"So the blood. . . ."

"Is just from a small head wound..."

"Are you okay?"

"I'm fine, just a little sticky," the uneasiness overtook her body once again.

"Are you up for grave digging?"

She paused and took a deep breath "Now even more than ever, now I know I have to do it. This isn't the end; it's going to be a long journey before we send these bastards back to where they belong. Digging up the graves is just the first part. I understand if either of you want to bail."

"You already know my answer," Josh said.

"I'm not one to back down from a fight . . . especially one that I helped start," Andy said, looking somberly toward the woods, where the cemetery lay.

"Well then, we've got some holy land to desecrate."

Chapter 8 – Grave Secrets

Silence enveloped Rylie as she stood above the grave, Andy on her left and Josh on her right. It was completely dark except for the moonlight filtering through the trees overhead. They each held a shovel in one hand, just staring at the two graves. They were too scared to make the first hole in the dry ground. Rylie took a deep breath and was about to push the tip of her shovel in when she heard a buzzing in her ear. She stopped and dropped the shovel, rubbing her ear.

"What's the matter?" Josh asked, stepping forward toward her.

"Nothing. My ear was just . . . nothing," she didn't want to bother them with what she was hearing in her head.

"Are you sure we should be doing this?" Andy asked, shivering and looking around nervously.

"This is the only way to get the counter-curse. We have to dig up the grave and find the box if we want to get rid of them."

"Will Judith and Edward notice if we start digging up their graves?"

"I'm guessing they'll feel it the minute I drive the shovel into the ground. They're going to be pissed, so we have to do it fast."

"Who's going to make the first break into the earth?" Josh asked reluctantly.

"I think I should do it. They're more likely to come after me anyway. I don't want either of you to get hurt. We've already seen what Edward is capable of," Josh stared at the ground as the memory of earlier crept into his head.

"Okay, if you're sure you want to," Andy said.

"I'm sure." She picked up the shovel. "You ready?"

She took a deep breath and in one quick motion drove the shovel into the ground. She paused for a second as nothing happened. Then all of the sudden there was a great wind that blew her hair to the side of her head. She knew she couldn't stop now. She lifted the dirt out of the grave and threw it to the side.

The wind continued to blow and she drove her shovel into the dirt again. She kept shoveling. Then she felt a great force attempt to knock her over; somehow, she maintained her balance. Josh and Andy were hurled backward. Rylie tried to look back but the wind was too strong to see anything. She couldn't see Josh or Andy and she got frightened. Something forced her to turn around and continue to dig.

Fear grew inside of her even though she knew that it was Mary trying to protect her; Rylie just wished that Mary could protect Andy and Josh also. Every so often she tried to stop digging to help them, but she couldn't. She couldn't move out of the act that seemed to last for hours as the shovel was driven over and over into the damp soil. She heard Josh yell and she panicked, but Mary wouldn't let her even turn around now. After her arms were sore and aching she thought she was nearing the casket. Her suspicions were confirmed as her shovel hit something hard. She squinted down into the grave and the little moonlight illuminated the mahogany top of the casket.

Another great force came upon her and this time it pushed her into the grave. Her body fell forward onto the casket, dirt erupting around her. She coughed violently as the dirt seeped into her throat. As she pushed herself onto her knees, she didn't take her eyes off of the casket. She brushed the dirt off, moved back, and opened it slowly. The creaks echoed around the silent woods. The wind started up again and it blew the dirt all around her and into her hair. Inside the casket was nothing but ashes and a small wooden box.

Her heart skipped a beat as she grabbed the box and opened it quickly. The paper inside was decaying and she could barely make out four words written in Latin: *Aeternitas Agitas ab Plutonis.*

She had no clue what it meant, and she really didn't care as long as it banished the spirits. Something dropped down on her back, and she lifted her head to see dirt falling around her, attempting to cover her. Her screams bounced around the grave as she threw her hands over her head. This was the time try to recite the counter-curse now, even if it didn't work.

The dirt was falling on her heavily; she struggled to stand up but fell back down onto the casket. It poured over her mouth and nose, making it hard for hard to breath, let alone recite anything. She coughed as the dirt seeped into her lungs, and then started to say the counter-curse.

"Aeternitas . . . Agitas . . . ab . . . Plutonis!" the words sputtered out of her mouth but was barely heard over the howling wind and the dirt falling into her face.

The wind came to an abrupt halt and the last bit of dirt fell on her. Everything was eerily silent, though she knew they couldn't be gone. It couldn't be that easy. Breathlessly, she investigated the grave around her and found that the dirt had filled up to her waist. The thought of how Andy and Josh had been thrown backward made her gasp as she remembered.

With difficulty she lifted herself out of the grave and scrambled onto the dirt. Darkness was all she could see as she pulled herself up to her feet. The moon was hidden behind thick clouds. Her eyes searched for any sign of Andy or Josh, but she couldn't see anything. The thumping of her heart pulsated in her ears as she walked deeper into the cemetery, listening for any movement or sounds but she heard nothing.

An owl hooted above her and she jumped. Her heart beat never slowed as she continued to walk among the graves. She heard a sound behind her and she whirled around to see nothing but darkness. The fear made her quiver to the point that her teeth chattered. She turned back around and continued to walk faster.

The tip of her foot got caught on something and she went flying forward onto the ground with a dull thump as her body hit the hard forest floor; she groaned. Holding her head, she slowly pulled herself to a sitting position. She saw what she had tripped over. A shovel was lying on the ground, blood on the tip of it. Her hands clamped over her mouth and she crawled backward away from it.

It had of be one of the guys' shovels; hers was back at the grave. Then again, it might be another mind game that Judith was playing on her. It seemed so real but so had the others. She stood up and inspected the darkness around nervously.

The moon emerged and revealed a decaying corpse hanging from the tree, a noose around its neck. It appeared to be a man, though she couldn't be sure. She was frozen in terror as she stared up at it with its black eyes falling out of its sockets and its large purple tongue hanging out crudely. It was dripping both blood and some other liquid onto the ground.

She stumbled backward and turned around. She started into a run. With a thud, she ran into someone. She shrieked.

"Rylie, it's me," Josh said. "Stop screaming."

112

Even though it was dark, she could just make out his features. She was relieved to see that he was all right.

"Are you okay?" she asked. "Where's Andy?"

"I'm fine, just a little banged up. I don't know where Andy is. We were thrown into the woods. All I remember was him yelling as someone or something was beating me with my shovel."

"Oh God, where could he be?"

"I don't know. All of the sudden the beating stopped. When I looked up, he was nowhere to be seen. Hopefully he ran back to the house."

"Hopefully, but I doubt it. I really pissed Edward off by touching his mother's grave; he tried to bury me alive."

"What? But you're okay?"

"Yeah, and I got the counter curse too," she said, holding up the piece of paper. She tucked it safely into her pocket. "I tried reciting it, but he ran off."

"Honestly I'm glad; I don't want you to be in any more danger than you have to. We should go find Andy and make sure he's all right."

"Yes, we need to find him," She said hastily and turned around, forgetting about the corpse hanging from the tree. Another scream escaped her mouth as she saw it again.

"What?" Josh asked as he looked up into the tree. "What is it? I don't see anything."

"You don't see it?" she asked. She was relieved; this meant it was just another mind game.

"No, what is it?"

"A dead man or woman. I don't know, it's too decayed. It's horrible."

113

"Rylie, it's not real. Remember that and it might go away."

She closed her eyes tightly and then opened them again. Above her the corpse was still there but her mind willed it to go away. Instead of disappearing, the decaying rope that was tied to the tree snapped and the corpse plummeted to the ground. It smashed into the dirt in front of her and she jumped back with a shriek.

"Rylie, it's not real!" Josh yelled at her as she clutched his arm. "Tell yourself that it's fake!"

"I'm trying, she won't let me!" she cried as she let go of his arm.

She shut her eyes so tightly she was afraid that her eyeballs would burst through her lids, and then wrenched them open. Her heart beat heavily as she saw that the body was gone. She breathed a sigh of relief and put her head on Josh's shoulder to catch her breath.

"You good now?" Josh asked as she straightened up.

"As good as I'm going to get. We've got to go find Andy before anything bad happens to him," she said, taking Josh's hand and pulling him farther into the darkness.

"Rylie, where are we supposed to look?" Josh asked as he followed her.

"I don't know, all I know is we have to find him!"

"I know, but let's be smart about this; we don't want to get hurt any more than we already are."

"I'll be careful later, Andy could be dying now!"

"I agree, but we have to be careful or we won't be able to help him at all."

They heard what sounded like someone moving over by a big oak tree. Rylie started running, letting go of Josh's hand. She reached the tree, but there was nothing under it or around it. She heard the sound again but it was coming from even farther into the woods. She ran after towards it, but once again found nothing.

She turned around in circles in the dark, looking for anything that might suggest that Andy was there. Her breathing was erratic as Josh ran up to her and put his hand on her back. She didn't know that it was him at first, so she jumped and let out a yelp.

"Rye, you have got to stop doing that," Josh said, peering into the darkness.

"I'll stop when you stop sneaking up on me. God, Josh. . . ." She walked farther into the darkness.

"Did you hear him? Is that why you ran off?"

"I thought so, but then it switched directions. I think she's playing with me again," she said as she frantically turned all around, then stopped abruptly.

"Rylie, what. . . ." Josh began.

"*Shhh*!" she whispered. "Do you hear that?"

"Hear what?"

"Footsteps."

He listened carefully. Sure enough, he heard soft footsteps. It sounded like they were coming from behind them. They both turned around but saw nothing, mostly because it was so dark.

"Do you think it's Andy?" Josh whispered.

"I don't know, maybe."

They started to walk toward where the footsteps were coming from, but they still didn't see anything. Then as quickly as he disappeared, Andy emerged from the darkness. He was running toward them, bent over and holding his side.

115

"Andy!" Rylie exclaimed as she rushed over to him. "What happened?"

"I . . . was attacked," he was breathing heavily.

"By what?" Josh asked.

"I don't know, it's . . . like it's invisible," he was having a hard time catching his breath, "It tried to kill me."

"It tried to kill all of us," Josh said.

"Did you . . . get what we need?" Andy asked as he stood up straight.

"Yeah, got it right here," she said, patting her pocket.

"Good, let's get the hell out of here," Andy started to walk forward.

Josh and Rylie were about to follow him when they heard a loud cracking sound. They all stopped where they were and searched around for the source of the sound. The sound grew louder and louder until it stopped. Rylie quickly realized what it was when a crashing sound followed. It was the tree that Andy was standing near; it was falling and falling fast.

Josh ran forward as Andy just stood there in horror. Josh dove onto Andy, knocking him down and away from the tree. The tree crashed just as Andy and Josh hit the ground inches away from the giant trunk. They both sat up and stared at the tree in horror.

Rylie ran over to them and stepped through the branches and over the tree. Andy's face was pale. Josh stood up and helped Andy to his feet, as Rylie walked over to them.

"Are you two okay?" she asked.

"Yeah, fine," Andy said. "Thanks to Josh."

"No problem," Josh said.

"I'd probably be dead if it weren't for you," Andy said, looking from the tree to Josh. "Thanks, man."

Andy held his hand out for Josh to shake and Josh shook it gratefully. Rylie sighed; she thought it was ridiculous that it took Josh saving Andy's life for Andy to think Josh was a good person. She rolled her eyes as they started to walk back toward the cemetery.

"You know, Josh, it seems I was wrong about you," Andy said.

"It's okay. What matters now is that we're all right and that it will be over soon."

"Hopefully," Rylie added to herself.

They reached the edge of the tree line and the moon was visible again. They looked into the cemetery and realized that they were almost at the worn path that led into the town. As they walked out into the cemetery, something caught Rylie's eye in the field of tall grass. It was as if someone was walking toward the cemetery, though only the top of his or her head was visible.

As the person got closer, Rylie realized that it was Matt. He had a frightened look on his face. Both Andy and Josh saw Matt coming toward them, and they stopped. Matt walked out of the grass, carrying a flashlight in one hand and a suitcase in the other. He shined the flashlight at them, to see who they were, and scoffed when he realized it was Rylie.

"Rylie, what the hell are you doing out here?" Matt said as he walked up to her.

"I could say the same thing about you," Rylie said, crossing her arms.

"Hey, I'm out here because I had to leave town. It was too chaotic for me."

"Hold up," Andy said, "What do you mean too chaotic?"

117

"I mean the town's in an uproar. Everything's being boarded up, people getting the hell out and causing major accidents. You'd swear there was a hurricane coming or something." He noticed they were all covered in blood and dirt.

"Did something else happen?" Rylie asked, ignoring that Matt was staring at her.

"How the hell did you get covered in blood? What the hell is going on here?" he exclaimed.

"We had a run in with. . . ."

"Rylie. . . ."

"No, Matt, listen to me. We were attacked by Judith and Edward Pascal. They tried to kill us twice. Once when I was at Josh's house, and then just now when we dug up Judith's grave."

"What? You dug up a grave!" he exclaimed. "You realize how much trouble you can get in for that?"

"Yes, we know, but if we didn't, we wouldn't be able to send Edward and Judith back into the amulet. Now that we have the counter curse, we can save the town and all this chaos will be over."

Matt stared at her as if she was insane. "Amulet, counter curse . . . what kind of shit is this?"

"It's true," Andy, said speaking up. "No matter how much you don't want to believe in spirits and the supernatural, they're here."

"Plus," Josh said, butting into the conversation, "Since we've all been targeted, and you're related to Rylie, you're in danger too."

"It's true, Edward did say that. . . ."

118

"All of you just need to shut your mouths; you've all gone fucking crazy!" Matt snapped, backing up slowly.

"Look, Matt," Rylie said, stepping forward. "You saw what happened back at the house, with the door."

"It was the. . . ."

"The wind?" Josh interrupted. "Yeah, that was my rationalization before I got attacked."

"You need to all just shut up," he said, continuing to back up.

"Fine, just go," Rylie said. "That's all you ever do anyway. Run away. Whenever things are not how you want them."

"Or maybe because everyone around here is insane!"

"That's okay, run," Rylie said sarcastically. "Get as far away from the town as you can, and then you can live with the guilt if we all end up dying trying to save everyone!"

"Maybe I will."

"Go then! Coward!"

He turned around and started to walk fast back to the town. Rylie knew that he wasn't really going to leave town, though she wouldn't put it past him to try. Still she didn't really understand why he was walking back through the graveyard rather than taking his car. None of it made sense; she just turned back to Josh and Andy. She started walking in front of them and Josh came on one side of her and Andy on the other. Josh put his arm around her and they walked down through the cemetery.

"Man, Matt is such an idiot," Rylie said angrily.

119

"Yeah, but it's best to forget about him, we've got enough crap to deal with," Josh said. "We need to get to the Pascal house and get these spirits out of here. The town is in big trouble."

"I'm scared to go into town, the way Matt was describing it," Andy said.

"Right now I'd rather have the town full of scared people then a town where everyone is gone because they're dead," Rylie said. "Josh, have you talked to your parents lately to make sure they're okay?"

"Called them right before the graveyard they're staying put at our house. Told them to stay there but didn't go into detail. Don't think they would believe the whole angry spirits thing."

"Yeah, well you saw my father is the same way. I just hope he went home right after work at the store," Rylie said as they approached Judith's dug up grave.

A shiver ran down Rylie's spine; she realized what she was going to do. She came to the scary realization that this could lead to her death, and that her father, Andy, and Josh could be caught in the crossfire.

She was now very aware that she was covered in blood. Somehow in all the rush of things it hadn't bothered her, but now that she thought about it, all she wanted to do was go home and shower.

Chapter 9 – Sunken

Rylie stepped into the shower and flinched as her bare feet touched the cold porcelain. She turned on the shower and watched as the water came cascading out of the showerhead. Once the temperature was just right, she stepped in. She quickly shut the shower curtain that she had put back up and sighed as the warm water ran down her body.

The blood washed off her and turned the water running down the drain red. She took the washcloth from the rack at the back of the shower and used it to wipe the dried blood off of her face and neck. After she was finished she put her face into the water and closed her eyes. A tingly sensation came over her body and ran from her head to her toes. Her attention was drawn to the shower curtain as if she expected someone to be on the other side.

Rylie turned back to the showerhead and as she did that same weird, tingly sensation came over her. As she glanced down at her feet she saw the bloody water starting to rise around her. The water was slowly creeping up the porcelain tub. Looking at the drain, she couldn't see through the red, murky water but it didn't look like the stopper was in. If it were, she would've seen the shadow. The water had reached her ankles now, and she bent down and daringly plunged her hand into the water, caressing the drain. The stopper was not there.

A lump formed in her throat while she pushed her fingers down the drain; there was nothing in it, not even hair. She stood back up and stepped back as the bloody water swirled around the bottom of her calf. There was a noise coming from outside of the shower curtain that sounded horribly like the door creaking open an inch. Her head jerked toward the door and a shadowy figure darted past the curtain.

121

Rylie stifled a scream and turned back to the tub, breathing hard. She held her breath; the only sound was the running water. Her heart beat hard in her chest; it was so loud the sound pulsated in her ears.

Time seemed to stand still. Even the sound of the water seemed to fade. Then without warning she felt her left foot being yanked forward by an invisible but strong force. It caused her to lose her balance and she came crashing down into the tub.

Her head hit the tiled wall and as she slid down; a bloody trail followed from her already seeping head wound. She lay there, sprawled out in the still rising bloody water, breathing as if she had been running. Her head hurt badly and she could feel warm blood dripping onto her neck. She tried to grip onto the edge of the tub to hoist herself up, but it was too slippery. The shadowy figure darted past again, this time to the right.

The hot water was still running, making it hard for her to breathe or see. As she tried to stand up, she was violently pushed down by the same invisible force. Nausea came over her as she went to move and couldn't. Edward was the one behind the curtain. He was the one holding her down and he had her just where he wanted her.

Her face twisted with horror as she saw the shower dial turning until it shut off. The excess water ran out of the faucet, but it came out a deep crimson. Her left arm twitched but she still was pinned down. A popping noise sounded in her ears and she turned her head up to see the shower curtain being ripped from its rings one by one.

Rylie tried to scream but nothing came out; she realized she couldn't even open her mouth. All she could do was watch. When there were only three rings left and she could see the rest of the bathroom, she saw that there was nothing there.

Two rings came off. Rylie held her breath as she waited for the last one, but nothing happened. There was a click as the overhead light shut off. Darkness surrounded her while she listened to last ring pop and the curtain rip. The curtain fell to the ground and Rylie glanced around desperately. There was a pale light coming from the millimeter of space beneath the door. All of a sudden she felt a hand clamp around her ankle; this time she screamed loudly and it echoed around the bathroom.

Another hand was on her thigh and she screamed again, louder. The hand that was on her thigh went away but then she felt it over her mouth. She struggled against him, but the more she struggled the harder he bore down on her. She hoped that Andy or Josh heard her and would come to her rescue.

Edward pushed her head into the water. It was so dark she couldn't see her hand in front of her face. She struggled, but Edward was too strong. She tried to cry out as he forced her head under water, his hands moving to her shoulders.

Her struggling sloshed the bloody water all over the bathroom as he held her under. She tried her best not to inhale any of it. She whimpered as she started to lose air and felt the murky water sloshing in her throat. Her eyes were open, but she couldn't see anything. All of a sudden the light must have turned on. Instead of darkness all around her all she saw was red. She sputtered, trying to surface for air.

Edward was still pressing down on her, and he seemed to push harder and harder. Then there was another force, going the other way, trying to pull her out of the water. As the two forces pulled in opposite directions, Rylie's head swam. Oxygen was being cut off from her brain. Then there was a great tug from someone else.

Rylie broke the surface, took a sweet breath of victory, but was then plunged back down into the water, left to gasp for air again. She jerked around in the water, plunging in and out. Someone was trying to save her, but they might end up killing her.

There was one strong tug that brought her up out of the water, over the tub, and onto the bathroom floor. She lay on her side, Josh next to her, also covered in the bloody water. She coughed violently and red water projected from her mouth. She still struggled to breathe and she looked around at everything that was starting to cloud over. Then she felt someone turn her over on her back and hit her chest with great force. This allowed the rest of the water in her lungs to come out, all over the bathroom floor.

The room came back into focus as she felt someone wrap her in a towel. She saw Josh, pulling her up to the sitting position against the wall. Rylie turned back to the tub just in time to see the last gallon of bloody water run back into the drain. The bathroom had diluted bloodstains everywhere from the struggle. Rylie leaned against the wall for support, clinging to the towel with her left hand, running her right through her hair.

"Rylie are you okay?" Josh asked, frantically trying not to look her nakedness while bloody water dripped from his hair.

"Yeah, I think so," she said, out of breath.

"Maybe you should just sit here for a while to catch your breath," Josh suggested, putting his hand on her cheek.

"Yeah," she agreed, nodding.

"I thought I had lost you," Josh said his eyes almost overflowing with tears.

He kissed her on the forehead, stood up, and turned to Andy. Josh and Andy both stepped outside of the bathroom. Rylie couldn't hear what they were saying, but she figured it was about her. It was at this point that Rylie was very aware that she was naked, even with the towel. Of course the first time he had to see her naked was this horrid experience. She very much wanted to put back on her clothes.

"Are you sure that we should continue with the plan?" Rylie heard Josh whispered to Andy. "She's come closer and closer to death the further we get into this. Any further and it'll kill her—can we risk that?"

"Yeah, I know what you mean; I've been thinking the same thing. But you know that Rylie would never stop, she's too invested in it. We all are," Andy whispered back. "The common good's at stake here. Plus if we don't go on with it, we'll all die, including Rylie."

"So what are you saying? That we should risk her to save the town?"

"I don't know," Andy said, "I care about her as much as you do and I don't want to lose her, but is her life more important than anyone else's?"

"Are you really saying that the town deserves to live more than she does?"

"No, I'm saying that we'll all die if we don't try, then it won't matter how or why she died because it would be for nothing."

"I guess you've got a point. I just don't want to lose her. I haven't even known her that long, but somehow I've fallen in love with her," Josh said.

"She has that effect on people," Andy admitted.

Rylie felt comforted as she listened to them talk. She stood up, using the wall for support, still gripping the towel in her left hand so it didn't fall off. Her breathing was returning to normal. She walked to the doorframe and stepped out into the hallway.

"Rylie," Josh said, surprised. "Should you be standing up? Are you. . . ."

125

"Josh, I'm fine. Don't worry about me so much," she said. "And as for abandoning the mission, I heard you talking . . . if there's one thing you guys aren't good at, it's whispering. I'm not going to abandon anything; we're going to finish what we started."

"But, Rylie. . ." Josh said stepping forward.

"No, we've come too far to turn around now. We can't just stand around and watch everyone, including us, die. I'd rather die for the cause, than die a cowardly death. If you two want to back down, be my guest, but I've got a job to do."

"I'm not backing down," Josh said plainly. "I wasn't going to. I was just trying to. . ."

"Protect me, I know. Don't worry, I can protect myself. Unless someone's trying to drown me in my bathtub," she added uneasily.

"That's exactly what I'm talking about. What if we weren't there to save you?"

"I don't know, but you were there, and I think Mary knew that. Otherwise, she would have stepped in. You two forget that I have supernatural help."

"Yeah, but. . . ."

"Josh, give it a rest, just let me get dressed so we can go kick some ghost. . ." Suddenly, all the lights went out. ". . .Ass. What the hell?"

She felt around in the dark and found Josh's hand. She squeezed it tightly and desperately tried to see what around her. She felt Andy place a hand on her back as they all breathed heavily, not knowing what to do.

"Where did I put that flashlight that I had?" Josh wondered aloud.

"Isn't it in the kitchen?" Andy asked. His voice came from Josh's other side.

"Yeah, come on." Josh started to walk toward the steps, but Rylie didn't move. "Rylie, what's wrong?"

"If Andy's over there, and you're next to me. . . ." She gulped. "Then whose hand is on my back?"

"It's a puzzle, isn't it?" A voice hissed from behind her.

Rylie screamed and ran toward the stairs with Josh. The hand was gone from her back, but she could swear she felt hot breath on her neck. They reached the steps and carefully ran down, holding onto the railing as they went.

They reached the bottom and they all stumbled onto the carpet. Rylie's towel started to slip, but she caught it and pulled it back up to her chest. They ran toward the kitchen, but then the front door opened. At the same time, the lights came back on. A dark figure stepped through the entryway.

They realized it was Mr. Bradford. He set his bags down in the foyer and eyed them angrily.

"What the hell is going on?"

"Look, Dad, I can explain," Rylie said. She stepped forward, letting go of Josh's hand.

"Why are you all wet and only wearing a towel? And why are you all wet, Josh?" Mr. Bradford roared.

"Dad, Josh saved me."

"Saved you from what?"

"Drowning in the tub. Look, I know you don't believe in ghosts and all of this supernatural stuff, but something tried to kill me. It tried to kill all of us."

"Rylie, what did I tell you?" his hands balled into fists; she had never seen him this angry.

"Dad, something is here in Summer's Hollow, something evil, and you know it. I know you can feel it. We know how to stop it."

"Rylie..."

"We found a spell that will send these spirits back to where they came from, but we have to go to the Pascal house to do it."

"You're not going anywhere," he said, "You are going to stay here."

"Dad, you have to let us go. Everyone in town is going to die if we don't do something about it. Edward and Judith Pascal are going to eat this place alive."

"Rylie, I'm your father and I'm telling you that there are no ghosts in this town!"

He shouldn't have yelled so loudly. Rylie knew that Edward and Judith were furious. The door behind him slammed loudly. One of the pictures that hung on the wall flew off and landed between her and her father. The glass smashed. It was a picture of their family when her mother had still been there.

"Dad, I don't think you should have said that," Rylie said quietly, as her father stared in horror at the smashed picture lying on the floor.

Pictures in their frames were now being thrown across the room, smashing against furniture and walls. Everyone had dropped to the floor and covered their heads. When there were no more pictures on the walls, Edward decided to start throwing DVDs from the rack next to the television. They sailed over Rylie, Andy, Josh, and her father's head as they cowered on the ground.

Silence engulfed the house. All of them slowly stood, looking around carefully, as if they expected more things to be hurled at them by the invisible force. Rylie instinctively grasped Josh's hand as they walked around the couch cautiously.

"What in God's name was that?" Mr. Bradford wondered.

"That would be two extremely pissed off spirits," Andy replied, and Mr. Bradford just glared at him.

"Look, something weird is obviously going on here. I'm not saying it has anything to do with any ghosts," her father added. For a moment, Rylie had thought he believed. "But it's obviously something and until I find out what's going on, you three aren't going anywhere."

"Dad, we can't stay here, we're sitting ducks. We know how to fix this situation. You have to let us go."

"No one is going anywhere," he said sternly.

"Dad, this is total crap!" Rylie said, outraged. "Every single person in this town is going to die if we don't do something! Do you want the blood of innocent people shed because you wouldn't let us stop them?"

"Rylie, that's enough! Go up to your room right now, put some clothes on, and stay there! Andy, you go up to your room. Josh, it might be best if you go home right now."

"We should stay together. Splitting up could mean our deaths."

"Josh, if you ever want to see my daughter again, I suggest you go," he ordered.

"Mr. Bradford, I want to stay and help. You just said you wanted us to stay here."

"Go home before I call your parents. If I know your father, he'll come right over and take you home himself."

"I. . . ."

"Go now!"

Josh grumbled to himself, flashed a pair of sad eyes at Rylie, and then walked toward the open door. "You're killing us all. Do you realize that?" Josh said as he closed the door behind him and walked out to his truck.

Rylie shot an angry look at her dad who just pointed upstairs and walked into the kitchen. Rylie turned to Andy, who looked both afraid and angry. They started upstairs.

"He doesn't know what he's doing. We need to stop Edward and Judith tonight or the town is history," Rylie commenting gripping the railing.

"Don't worry," Andy whispered as they reached the top of the stairs. "We'll get to the Pascal house tonight, with or without your father's permission."

"Wow, you're never one to blatantly disobey my father."

"The circumstances are dire, plus he'll thank us later when he's still alive."

She smiled at Andy and then walked up the hallway and into her room. She closed the door and dropped her wet, blood-stained towel to the floor. She crossed her room to her dresser where she pulled her bra, underwear, and socks out of the bottom drawer. She pulled them all on, then went into her top draw and selected a pair of dark blue jeans that she put on over her black underwear. The closet door was open and it made her shiver. It was as if Edward was in the closet watching her. Reluctantly, she went to the closet and picked out her Metallica T-shirt, then closed the door fast.

Her semi-wet brown hair dripped slightly as she pulled it up into a ponytail and walked over to her bed. She sat down on her bed and put her head in her hands. She was so tired of all this. She was tired of watching her back, tired of having to be the strong

130

one, tired of her father not believing her, and tired of her brother being an ass. More than anything, she was scared out of her mind. She had almost been killed a number of times and now that Josh was on his own, she feared for his life as well. She knew that she had to get out of this house and get to the Pascal House before anything bad happened.

Her cell phone rang and she jumped up and grabbed it. She picked it up after the first ring and put the receiver to her ear.

"Hello?" she said, shaking slightly.

"Rylie, it's me," Josh said. She breathed a sigh of relief.

"Josh, good, I was going to call you. Look, we need to get out of this house and to the Pascal House, tonight. Where are you?"

"Don't worry; I'm just around the corner. You really think I was going to leave you there? I'll come pick you and Andy up. You think you can sneak out?"

"Yeah, just stay where you are so my dad can't see you and we'll sneak out the window."

"Okay, I'm just around the corner, parked in the woods. Be careful and I'll see you in a little bit."

"You be careful too, and keep your eyes open at all times. I'll see you," she said and then hung up the phone fast. Andy opened the door to her room, walked in, and shut it behind him.

"We've got to go now. Josh is waiting for us. That was him on the phone," Rylie explained.

Rylie located the yellowed piece of paper that had the spell written on it and quickly shoved it into the pocket of her jeans. She then grabbed her brown shoulder bag that was

131

already full of flashlights and candles from earlier. The night air rushed into her room as she opened the window and threw her bag over her shoulder.

"Ladies first," Andy said as Rylie carefully climbed onto the ledge below the window. "And don't look down."

Chapter 10 – Belief

Rylie and Andy quietly crept across the lawn towards the woods. They reached the dirt path and spotted Josh's truck sitting there, the motor still running. Rylie glanced back at the house for a second to make sure that her father hadn't noticed that she and Andy were gone. Andy put his hand on her back to hurry her up. She took the hint and picked up speed so that they quickly reached the truck. As soon as both she and Andy clambered into the truck, Josh took off down the road.

"We'd better get away from your house before your dad finds out that you guys are gone," Josh said as he headed up the dark road.

"Yeah, he's going to be pissed once he finds out we're gone. Now it's not a matter *if* he finds out, it's *when*," Rylie said as she set down the bag next to her.

"I got a call from Brian; he said that he and Alec wanted to come along and help. I tried to convince them not to come, but they feel like they owe it to Luke."

Rylie nodded as they turned off the dirt road and onto the main one that led into town. She thought about whether or not she was really prepared to face Edward and Judith head on, if she could suppress her fear enough to do it. Her head pounded from all the stress that she had gone through the past few days and all the fear that had overtaken her. She wondered if she would be able to return to her normal life. She hoped that she wouldn't always be afraid something would be lurking around every corner.

She felt the truck stop and she looked up to see Brian's house. Brian and Alec rushed out; Brian had a black backpack across his left shoulder. They got into the backseat of the truck but Josh didn't say anything to them. He just waited until they closed the door, and then headed for the Pascal house.

133

Rylie turned to Andy, who smiled nervously at her, then looked back out the window at the still night. No wind blew, no animals made any sounds, and the moon was casting an ominous glow from behind the thin gray clouds. As they entered the woods, Rylie's stomach plummeted to her feet. She felt a chill and had the strong feeling that something incredibly bad was going to happen. This time it wasn't Mary communicating to her, it was her own intuition.

They took the fork in the road. As they approached the looming Pascal house, the engine died.

"What the hell?" Josh hit the brakes.

He turned the key and the starter clicked, but the engine failed to turn over. He tried again, but nothing happened. Everyone groaned in annoyance, but Rylie knew this was no coincidence. She glanced over at the instrument panel and saw all the needles going crazy as if they were part of a seismograph. A loud high pitch screech came blasting out of the speakers and seemed to echo around the truck. They all clamped their hands over their ears.

"I'll get out and check what's wrong," Josh said as the screech subsided. Rylie grabbed his hand.

"Josh, I don't think this is just a problem with the truck. It could be what he wants: you out in the night, where he can attack you."

"Rylie, I'll be fine. You stay here. Hand me a flashlight; I'll just be a second," he said. Reluctantly, she handed him the flashlight.

Andy opened the door and stepped out. "I'll come with you."

They both shut the doors and walked around to the hood. Josh opened the hood, blocking Rylie's view of them; this made her all the more uncomfortable. Brian and Alec were silent in the back seat, their faces still full of grief and pain. This was the first time she had seen them since Luke's death and it was clear that they were apprehensive to be here despite what they had told Josh. Rylie could hear the sound of Andy and Josh talking, but she couldn't make out the words. Whatever it was, it didn't sound good. Her nostrils filled with the sharp smell of gasoline.

"Oh, shit," Josh said as he opened the driver's side door. "You all need to get out now!"

They scrambled out of the truck and into the dark night. Once Rylie was out, she could see gas spewing out of the tank and all over the dirt road. It was clear this wasn't something normal that happened and soon the edges of her shoes were wet with gasoline.

"One spark and the whole truck could catch fire," Andy said as they all stepped back.

"That's just what he wants," Rylie said as Josh held her arm. "He wants to take us out fast and easy. I told you we didn't just break down out of nowhere."

"Maybe we should go into the house now and just leave the truck," Josh suggested.

"Wait," Andy said. "Did you hear that?"

"Hear what?"

"It sounded like a strike, like someone. . . ." There was a roaring sound.

"Move!" Josh yelled, pushing Rylie down the road and the others followed.

They looked back as the truck erupted in flames. Then without warning an explosion rocked the countryside and they all ran farther down the road. The night was lit up by an orange glow emitting from what was left of the truck. They all stood still in shock at the explosion as the truck still emitted fire and smoke behind them. As flames engulfed the truck, they all turned around and noticed that they were covered in soot from the explosion.

"That's going to alert the whole town, what's left of them anyways, and they're going to come see what happened," Rylie said. "That includes my dad, who has probably figured out we're gone. So we better go and take care of this fast."

"How the hell does that even happen? ...Wait a second," Andy stopped. "Wasn't the spell in your bag that was in the truck?"

"No, I put it in my pocket, but the flashlights and candles were in my bag."

"We have one flashlight," Brian finally spoke up and handed it to Josh.

"But we have five people, it's not going to do a lot of good," Rylie pointed out.

"We'll just have to stick together, okay?" Josh said, rubbing her arm.

"Let's go." Rylie took a deep breath and led them toward the house.

Josh followed, holding her hand. Andy walked behind them. Alec and Brian hesitated for a second, but then followed them across the grass, leaving the flame-engulfed truck behind them. The five of them reached the infamous front steps that they had stood on less than two days ago.

This time, Josh was the brave one. He let go of Rylie's hand and opened the creaky old door. It swung open to reveal the dusty house. They hesitated, but eventually they all made it into the foyer.

Dust hung in the air; Rylie felt it on her skin and in her hair as stood there. None of them dared to go any farther at the moment. It was dark, and she couldn't see much.

136

What she could see was the kitchen where Luke had died. Rylie noticed that both Alec and Brian were avoiding the kitchen at all costs. They had good reason to.

As her eyes adjusted to the dank light, they all started forward, very slowly. It was as if they expected to be attacked the moment they stepped toward the stairs. Rylie and Josh, who had already endured the wrath of the Pascals, were the first ones to climb the staircase.

The others followed them cautiously. Rylie just wanted this to be over with. She had been through so much already; it was tearing her family and her friends apart. She was glad Sarah was not here; at least she knew that one of her friends was out of harm's way.

They reached the top of the stairs and Rylie started toward the attic. This was where she knew she had to go. She couldn't explain it; she just knew that this was where it would end. They continued into the musty, dark attic that gave Rylie the chills more than any other part of the house. None of them knew what to do; they waited for direction from Rylie.

She needed something that would force the Pascals into the attic so that she could recite the spell. She wished she had Mary's diary; a passage within it might have shed light on the situation. Then something occurred to Rylie. She and Mary were psychically connected. If Mary could tap into Rylie, why couldn't Rylie tap into Mary? Especially since Mary was somewhere in the house right now.

Not really knowing how to achieve her goal, she closed her eyes and concentrated on Mary. A strange sensation came over her. Coldness swept into her chest and it felt as though thousands of tiny insects were crawling all over her. The sensation began at her legs and worked its way up the rest of her body. Then she lost control of her body again and felt herself walk over to one of the many chests.

"Rylie, what are you doing?" Josh asked.

She couldn't answer; Mary wouldn't let her talk. This was most likely because Josh wouldn't like what Mary was doing, or what Rylie was doing. Mary made Rylie open the chest. She pulled out of piece of what looked like charcoal and a small hatchet.

"Rylie, answer me!" Josh exclaimed. He looked terrified and with good reason. She saw in the reflection of the floor length mirror that her eyes had turned from the usual hazel to a bright green

Mary then took the charcoal, bent down to the ground, and touched it to the wooden floor. She drew a big circle with a diameter of about five feet. Inside she drew a bunch of weird symbols that she didn't recognize, but Rylie figured it was some kind of spell.

She threw the charcoal to the side as everyone else just watched her, too stunned to know what to do. She took the hatchet in her hands and held it as if she were about to hit something with it. As they all watched fearfully, she walked over to one of the wooden walls, buried the hatchet into the wall, and pulled it out. She hit the wall again; coldness filled the room, along with the stench of death.

The cold sensation left Rylie and she almost fell to the floor as she regained control of her body. She figured out what Mary had done. It was a binding spell she had drawn on the floor so the Pascals couldn't leave. The hatchet had drawn them here since it was changing their environment and they didn't like that. Now they were stuck in the attic.

There was a yell from behind Rylie. She turned to see Alec thrown against the wall. He stayed there, his feet inches from the ground. Brian ran over to him and tried to pull him down, but he couldn't get him to budge. Rylie pulled out the piece of paper with the curse on it and started to read it. The flashlight in Josh's hand went out and they stood there in the murky darkness.

There was another yell and a crash but Rylie couldn't tell where it was coming from. All of a sudden, her feet left the ground. She flew through the air, hit the hard floor, and slid across it and into the wall. She heard a scream, but it was a woman's voice and she didn't understand it.

"Rylie, read it!" Andy yelled.

"I'm trying, I can't see anything!" she screamed. As soon as she said it, the moon moved from behind the clouds and a single beam of light fell onto the floor from out the window.

She sought the beam of light so she could see, and shouted out, "Aeternitas . . . Agitas . . . ab . . . Plutonis!"

All of the sudden there was a flash of light and a burning in her chest as the amulet seemed to absorb the light. She clutched her chest in pain and sunk lower to the floor. It subsided as quickly as it started. Rylie breathed heavily, trying to catch her breath. The guys stayed where they were; the sounds of their shallow breathing were the only thing anyone heard.

It was over. Everything they had been through was over and yet it was over so quickly. Rylie thought back to how complicated getting to this point had been. It seemed way too easy and didn't sit well with her. Something still didn't feel right. She sat on the ground, waiting for something else to happen.

"Rylie," Josh said, helping her off the ground and putting his arm around her. "It's over, let's go. . . ."

She didn't say anything. She couldn't shake the feeling that it wasn't over. She could feel it in her gut as Josh steered her out of the house along with the others. They walked out onto the lawn and took a last glance at the house. It looked the same as it always did with its chipped paint and rotting wooden but it now had a sinister look to it. It was in her mind that if they got rid of Judith and Edward, the house would look different, but it didn't.

"Well I for one will never be setting foot in that house ever again," Andy said, breaking the silence.

"I completely agree." Josh pulled Rylie close to him.

"Something's not right," Rylie said as they turned around and walked back to the road. "It's not over."

"What are you talking about?" Josh asked. "You're the one who said that cursing them back into the amulet would stop it. What happened up in the attic seemed like it worked."

"Yeah, I know they're in there, that's not the problem. I just don't feel like it's over."

"Maybe you have that feeling because it's been going on for so long now."

"Maybe," Rylie said as they walked down the dirt road.

They saw what was left of the truck, still smoldering. Josh sighed. She knew that Josh probably loved that truck, and it pained him to see it in ruins. He pulled away from her momentarily and she squeezed his arm with affection.

"Wait, Josh, something's wrong," Rylie said, stopping in her tracks.

"Rylie?"

"No, something's definitely wrong," she yelled. "Look at your truck! That explosion was huge; it would have been heard in town. It would've been seen, even from a distance."

"Yeah, I know."

"Then why is no one here?" Rylie said frantically. "Where are the police? Where are the fire fighters? Huh?"

"Rylie's got a point there," Andy said gravely.

"Maybe they couldn't see it because of the trees," Josh suggested.

"But someone would have heard it," Rylie insisted. "Can we please go into town and make sure that everything's alright?"

"Fine, but I don't know how we're going to get there."

"We'll do what I used to do all the time to get to school," she decided. "We'll cut through the cemetery."

"Well that's a happy thought," Brian muttered.

"It's all over, so it doesn't matter, right? We're safe," Andy said, but he didn't sound like he believed it.

"I don't know," Rylie said. "The spirits are gone, but I just have this feeling in the pit of my stomach that something's still wrong."

"Like what?"

"Like something's wrong in town," she said as they started to walk up the road that led into the woods.

"Rylie, I think you're overreacting. It should be over," Josh said.

"Yeah, sure, overreacting…"

They walked in silence through the woods until they reached the cemetery. Rylie held onto Josh's hand tightly and at first didn't want to step into the cemetery. At one point she even thought she heard the word *don't* whispered into her ear.

"Come on, Rylie," Josh said. "It was your idea to go into town."

"I know." She took a deep breath and started to walk forward into the dark cemetery. The others followed.

They walked all walked quickly through the cemetery. The hair on Rylie's arm was sticking up the entire time but she pressed on. They finally emerged from the woods and started into town. Once again the eerie silence crept into every corner. Instinctively, Rylie headed for the police station. Her friends followed without question.

All the lights were on at the station, but it didn't seem like anyone was in there. She pushed open the glass door and walked through the waiting room to the front desk. She saw no one; the uneasiness that was growing inside of her was growing within her friends as well.

"Hello?" she called. "Anyone here?"

There was no answer so Josh walked around the counter and into the back where all the officers' desks were. Rylie poked her head around to look and she heard Josh calling out for anyone with no response. She couldn't understand where everyone was. Something sitting behind a desk next to the phone caught her eye. It was a sketch artist's rendition of a wanted man—the drawing was a dead ringer Edward Pascal. Under the picture there were notes:

Man in early 40s, Six Feet, Suspect name: Possibly Edward?

"Holy crap," she mumbled to herself.

"What?" Andy asked, coming up behind her and looking at the paper.

"Apparently we weren't the only ones in town to run into Edward." She sighed. "Someone must have come in and gave a description to whoever drew this."

"Is that bad?" Andy asked uncertainly. "The police have a suspect now. They have someone to blame for the murders. Isn't this what you wanted? For everyone to realize that it was Edward and Judith, not Mary? That they had come back and killed people? That their spirits were released?"

"I don't know, I guess." Nothing was right about this.

Suddenly they heard Josh yell from the back room. Both Andy and Rylie rushed to find him, followed closely by Brian and Alec. They found Josh near the holding cells. What he was looking at turned her stomach.

In the one holding cell were what appeared to be three officers. It was hard to tell since they were unrecognizable: hacked beyond belief. Blood seemed to cover every surface in the cell. Some of it was still wet and running down the walls. Rylie turned to Josh, horrified and on the verge of vomiting.

"See, it's not over yet," she said, her voice shaking.

"This . . . this could've happened before we sent Edward and Judith back into the amulet," Josh retorted.

"Josh, the blood is fresh. This just happened," she said, her heart beating fast.

"Oh, so now you're an expert?" Andy asked. His eyes watered, he was pale, and he looked like he was about to puke. "We don't know that for sure. But how do we explain how it happened? Edward and Judith are in that amulet." He pointed to the pendant around her neck. "How could they still be killing?"

"Wait a second," Rylie said. "The curse."

"What curse?" Josh asked, walking away from the bloody scene.

"The curse on the town. I read in Mary's diary that when Judith died, she cursed the town. That's why for thirteen years after Mary died, people were dropping like flies. I was confused about why they suddenly stopped dying. I thought that it was because they were cursed into the amulet. But I forgot that Mary cursed them into the amulet before she died. So for those thirteen years both Edward and Judith were stuck in that amulet."

"Wait, now I'm confused. What are you talking about?" Andy asked.

"Judith said right before she died that as long as people believed in the supernatural that both she and Edward would still have power."

"So what? The curse relies on people believing in them?" Andy asked.

"Exactly," Rylie said proudly. "For thirteen years, the legend of Edward and Judith Pascal was alive and well, even though they were packed away in the amulet. The fact that people believed in them brought them to life. The reason that the killings stopped is people stopped believing in them. They lost all their power."

"People believed the legend in modern times," Brian said, finally opening his mouth. "You believed it, others believed it too. So why have the killings started just now?"

"But it wasn't the same legend. You know how urban legends work, it's all word of mouth, and the story tends to change along the way. Sometime between May 3, 1788 and

144

today, the storylines got crossed and Mary replaced Edward and Judith as the killer. Yes, we believed it, but Mary was never a killer." then she realized something. "We were *better off* thinking Mary was the killer. When we released Edward and Judith and started to believe in them, the curse manifested itself again. And when I was going around and trying to get people to believe that they were back, I was throwing fuel on the fire. Now that people have seen Edward and that sketch of him is out there, the fire is blazing."

"So to break the curse, people have to stop believing in them?" Andy asked.

"Easier said than done," Josh pointed out. "People aren't just going to stop believing."

"There has to be another way," Rylie said. "In a spell like this, there's usually some point of amplification that focuses the beliefs of the people onto the curse."

"Whoa," Josh said, surprised. "How the hell did you know that?"

"Um, I didn't," she didn't get it but then it clicked, "But Mary did. I told you we were connected."

"If that is true, where is this amplification point?" Andy wondered.

"It has to be somewhere that Edward and Judith would have power, where people would go regularly, especially in the past few days. . . ." She paused. "Right! The museum."

Suddenly, all the lights went off in the police station. "That can't be good," Andy whispered.

"We need to get the hell out of here," Rylie said as her eyes adjusted to the darkness and she started off running.

"Rylie!" Josh called after her, and quickly followed.

Chapter 11 – Blame

"Rylie," Josh said, breathing heavily as he caught up with her at the museum. "Don't go running off like that in the dark."

"Sorry, but I think I figured it out." She tried to open the museum doors, but they wouldn't budge. "Dammit, we're going to have to break the glass."

"Great, so we break the glass and alert them to where we are," Josh said.

"News flash, Josh: they already know where we are. Speaking of which, where are the other guys?"

Josh turned around to peer down the dark street and saw no one. "I don't know, I thought they were right behind me."

"Go make sure they're okay. Edward and Judith could've gotten them," she said, panic creeping into her voice.

"I'm not leaving you alone," Josh said sternly.

"I'll be fine, now go!"

"All right, but be careful." He hesitated but then turned around and headed back to the police station.

Rylie tried again to open the door, but it wouldn't budge. She glanced around and found a rock over on the road. Then she covered her face with one hand and hit glass hard with the rock. The glass didn't break that easily so she had to hit it twice more and then it broke. It was a big enough hole that she could stick her hand through to unlock the door. She opened the door expecting the alarm to go off, but it didn't.

It was strange but she kept going in spite of it. There was no clue or indication of what to look for but she figured whatever it was would be here. She walked over to the book with all the artifacts in it and started to flip through it, looking for anything that might help her. It was mostly useless stuff like the different clothes they wore or the utensils they used. Then she came across an entry for a book. It was supposedly a book of spells that belonged to Mary, but Rylie bet that it really belonged to Judith.

Rylie searched around through the artifacts that were in the glass cases in the museum. She saw the book in a case with some other artifacts. She broke the glass case with an old pitchfork from a display and picked up the book. Everything felt too easy, and it occurred to her that Mary was helping her along, ensuring that nothing interrupted her. Rylie flipped through the book until she found the spell she was looking for.

Eidolonic Necromancy: Creation of a thought form through magical amplification. Specifically the manifestation of spirits through intensified visualizations.

After the short entry, there was a symbol. The symbol looked almost like a Celtic knot but instead of being circular the parts of the knot were more diamond like. Below it there was a caption that identified it as the "Tibetan Infinite Symbol." She knew that she had seen that symbol somewhere before; this worried her because it meant that other people had seen it too.

Guilt crept into her the more she discovered. It was her fault; if she had just left the amulet alone, none of this would've happened. If she had kept her mouth shut about discovering the truth about Mary and Edward, nothing would have happened. She wanted everything to go back to normal.

She thought of Josh and the others and turned to leave the museum. As she walked out the door, she ran into a dark figure and screamed as she backed up. Then she realized who it was.

"Matt!" she exclaimed. "What are you doing?"

"Trying not to get killed." His expression showed that he was just as frightened as Rylie. "What are you doing in town?"

"Trying to get rid of the spirits," she said fearfully.

"And how do we do that?" he asked. Apparently, he had changed his mind about Edward and Judith Pascal.

"I think we have to destroy this symbol," she said, showing him the passage in the book. "And since when are you so quick to believe me? It was not so long ago you thought I was crazy and wanted to get as far away from me and this town as possible."

He swallowed hard. Even in the dark, she could see that his face was full of terror. "After I witnessed three cops being slaughtered, I think I've come around on the subject."

"Whoa, you were in the police station when those cops got torn apart?" she exclaimed.

"You saw them? Oh shit, Rye, I wish you didn't have to see that, but yeah I was there. I was in the cell. They thought I was acting suspicious, and thought I was involved in the murders. Boy, were they off."

"We have to go back to the police station. Josh, Andy, Alec, and Brian are all there. They could be in trouble!" She started in that direction, but Matt grabbed her arm to stop her as he turned back to the book.

"What are you doing?" she exclaimed. "We have to go find them! What? What's the matter?" She turned and her eyes focused on the clock tower. On the tower was the Tibetan Infinite Symbol. "Holy crap."

"So what? We have to destroy it?" Matt asked.

"Uh huh. I don't know how, though."

"I know," he said as he took her hand and pulled her toward the tower.

"Wait, what about the others?"

"If what you say is true and we destroy this, they should be fine. We have to hurry," Matt said, pulling her along.

Something about this made her uncomfortable. Why was Matt so willing to help and believe everything she said without questioning it? He pulled her to the tower and let go of her to try to break the lock on the door. It took him a handful of attempts but eventually the wooden door flew open, revealing the steps up to the clock. Matt started up, but Rylie hung back.

"Rye, come on!"

It wasn't like him to go along with whatever he was told, especially if it came from her "How exactly are we going to destroy it?" she asked, testing him.

"The tower's made of wood. So we can just burn it down," he said simply. "Now, come on and help me."

"No," she said, crossing her arms over her chest. "Something's not right."

"Rylie, come on," He took her by her arm and pulled her hard.

"Ouch, Matt, you're hurting me," she said as he practically dragged her up the stairs.

He ignored her protests and continued to pull her until they reached the landing. Then he let go of her and she stumbled to the ground. She stood up and saw Matt looking around the tower.

"What are you doing?" she asked. "Just light it on fire and let's get out of here."

"Actually, there's been a change of plans," he said. They both turned towards the wall, where the other side of the symbol was clearly visible.

"What the hell are you talking about? Matt, what's going on?" she saw his lips curls into a sneer, "You're not Matt, are you?" she said meekly.

"You know, Rye, I thought you'd be a lot smarter than that. You figured everything else out. You'd think that you wouldn't fall for the old possession trick twice." He laughed.

"Edward," she said with loathing. "Where are my friends?"

"Don't worry; you'll be joining them soon. First, I must thank you." He clapped his hands. "If it weren't for you, I'd still be stuck in that stupid amulet. When you convinced everyone else that we were running around killing people, it was quite good for us."

"Bite me, you murdering bastard," she spat.

"Watch it, sweetheart, I just might." He laughed and lifted his hand. She was thrown against the wall and pinned there.

"I swear if you hurt any of my friends or my family. . . ." She spoke through clenched teeth.

"You're going to what? Kill me?" He laughed. "Sorry to break it to you, but I'm already dead."

"Then I'll send you to hell where you belong."

"Come on, we know that as long as people believe in us, as long as even a *handful* of people believe in us, hell is the last place that we're going to be."

"So where's mommy dearest?" she asked mockingly. "Doesn't she want to join in on the fun?"

"Oh, she's having her own fun," he said conspiratorially.

"So it's been more than two hundred years and you're still a momma's boy, huh?" Rylie spoke in the same mocking tone; Edward seemed to despise it.

He moved his hand again and she flew through the air and slammed into the back of the clock. As she picked herself up off the ground, she had an idea. She grabbed the clock turner and turned it to the next hour so that the clock started to chime. Edward put his hands over his ears as Rylie scooted across the floor to retrieve the book. He stumbled over to her and threw her toward the opening in the tower.

She was hanging out of the tower and could see the ground below. There were distant figures that looked like Josh, Andy, Brian, and Alec rushing toward the tower. Her lips curled into a weak smile as Edward advanced on her. He picked her up by her neck, pulled her away from the opening, and slammed her back into the wall. Footsteps resounded below them. This turned Edwards's attention away from her momentarily.

Josh came running up the stairs and Edward sent him flying into the other wall while still holding Rylie by the neck. Rylie decided to bite down on his arm. Edward dropped her onto the floor and yelped in pain. Andy leapt at Edward, knocking them both through the opening in the tower.

"Andy!" Rylie yelled after him and ran toward the opening.

Her stomach was in her throat and she daringly glanced down to see Andy clinging onto the ledge. Edward was holding onto Andy's ankle. Rylie yelled for Josh and he rushed over and tried to help Andy up off the ledge. Andy didn't make it easy for Josh since he was thrashing around trying to shake Edward off of him. Rylie wanted this to end but she knew that if Edward fell, so would Matt and her brother would be dead.

"Andy, be careful!" Rylie called as Josh pulled Andy up onto the ledge.

Edward lunged forward onto the ledge and Andy instinctively shoved him off. His eyes grew wide as he realized what he had done.

"No!" Rylie screamed as she watched her brother's body fall through the air and hit the ground with a sickening thud. "Matt!"

Rylie sobbed and started to run toward the stairs, but Josh caught her.

"Rylie, wait! Edward could still be in him. How do we destroy this symbol?"

"It's on the side of the tower," she said as tears fell down her face. "The only thing we can do is burn the tower down."

"Okay." He tried to remain calm while he held her by the shoulders so that she didn't go running off. "Does anyone have a lighter?"

"Yeah," Brian said distantly as he pulled one out of his pocket.

"You two stay here," Josh said to Brian and Alec. "Andy, come on, we're going to find some gasoline or something for accelerant."

Brian and Alec nodded and Josh let go of Rylie and started to hurry out of the tower and down the stairs. Before he could stop her, Rylie was running down the stairs two at a time, almost falling when she reached the bottom.

"Rylie!" he yelled after her.

She ignores him, ran towards Matt's body, and fell to her knees next to him. "Oh, God." She cried as she put her hand over her mouth. "No, no . . . Matt . . . God, it's all my fault."

"Rylie!" Josh called out again as he rushed over to her out of breath. Andy was running to the gas station that was a block down the street. "Rylie, get away from him!"

Rylie didn't listen; she put her hand in Matt's hair and cried. "Matt, I'm so sorry. I didn't want it to end this way." She sobbed.

Blood was on her hands as she doubled over Matt and cried for her brother. Then all of a sudden, Matt's body started to twitch. She saw this, stopped crying, and sat up. Her brother began to convulse. She didn't know what to do; she didn't know if this was her brother or if it was Edward trying to get out. Her question was answered when Matt's eyes snapped open and he sat up. That same sneer flashed across his face and she knew that it was Edward.

"Get out of my brother, you son of a bitch!" she yelled, tears stinging her eyes.

"Sweetheart, I'm the only thing that's keeping your brother alive right now." Edward laughed as he took her by the hair and slammed her head into the ground.

"Rylie!" Josh yelled again as he launched himself on top of Edward.

Edward lazily tossed him to the side with a flick of his hand and then stood up, laughing. Rylie laid face first in the road, moaning in pain. She tried to push herself up but all she could do was remain doubled over on her knees.

"You two kids don't give up, do you?" Edward laughed. "Come on, now . . . It's over! We've won, we control this town now. All the cowards left and the people that

153

stayed behind are boarded up in their homes. The law doesn't know what to do. Chaos has ensued in Summer's Hollow and we love it!"

"You haven't won yet, Edward!" Josh yelled, moving toward him.

Rylie's turned and saw Andy running back down the street out of breath with a bottle of liquor in his hand that Rylie assumed he stole from the liquor store down the street. A slight smile crossed her lips as she turned back to Josh and gave him a keep-Edward-talking look. Josh saw this and nodded at her.

"Really? Because I do believe we have," Edward said. "I'm still stuck in that amulet, but our little town fears us again, and that keeps our legend alive."

"But if your legend was alive, why can't you manifest yourself?" Josh retorted. "You're still using other people to do your dirty work. Guess you're not as powerful as you thought you were."

Edward didn't like this taunt. He brought Josh toward him with his hand and picked him up by his neck. "Still think I'm not that powerful, you little vermin?" Edward sneered.

"I'll be impressed when you can do this in your own form." Josh struggled to speak as he tried to push Edward's arms away.

"In due time, in due time." Edward smiled.

"I don't think so." Rylie used all her strength to stand up.

"Really?" Edward laughed as he turned to her. "And what makes you say that?"

"That." Rylie nodded up at the tower.

154

"What. . . ." Edward turned and saw flames leaping up the tower as Brian, Alec, and Andy rushed down the stairs just in time. Flames exploded from the openings in the tower.

Edward dropped Josh to the ground. Josh was breathing heavily and clutching his throat. "It's over, Edward."

"It's finally over. You have no power anymore," Rylie said.

Edward sunk to his knees and gaped as flames leapt over the symbol, blackening it. "No!" he yelled, and then turned back to Rylie. "You're just like her! You bitch!"

"I'll take that as a compliment." Rylie watched as Edward squirmed and pulled at his stolen skin.

"You're wrong, though," he said, panting. "The symbol, it just amplified the curse. As long as. . . ." He could barely speak now as his body seized with pain. "People believe in us . . . just a couple of people . . . we'll still be . . . around. . . ." With his last breath, he fell over and a weird flash of light erupted from Matt's body.

Rylie watched as Matt crumpled for the last time. She wept as she heard sirens in the distance. She knew that the curse was broken for the most part but Edward was right. As long as people believed in them they would still have *some* power. She knew what she had to do to ensure that no one would ever believed in Edward and Judith again. *Someone else* had to be blamed for the murders.

Tears spilled down her cheeks as she looked at her brother's dead body. Josh walked over, still rubbing his neck, and he put his arm around her. Andy, Brian, and Alec surveyed Matt's body with sadness in their eyes. Police cars were pulling up, along with two fire trucks.

"It's over now," Andy said, still looking at Matt's body. "I mean . . . *really* over?"

Rylie nodded. Josh seemed confused. "But I thought Edward said. . . ."

"No, it's really over," Rylie interrupted as the police rushed over to them, guns drawn.

"What happened?" one of the officers asked.

"It was Matt," Rylie said firmly. "It was him." Her friends stared at her as though she was crazy.

"I thought he was in a holding cell?" the other officer asked as more flames exploded from the tower.

"Come on, we need to move away from the tower!" one of the officers yelled. "It's going to collapse!"

Sure enough, just as they rushed away, the top of the tower started to lean to one side and fell onto the ground right where Matt's body was. Rylie's heart ached for her brother, but she knew that she had to do the right thing for the safety of the people.

The firefighters were readying the hoses as people emerged from their houses to watch the spectacle. Rylie hugged Josh tightly as she cried into his shirt. Josh hugged her back and placed his hand on the back of her head.

"We need to get you kids to the station so that we can get your statements," one of the officers said.

"And you're sure that your brother is responsible for the murders?" another man asked.

156

"Yes," Rylie said crying, "He told me everything right before . . . right before he jumped out of the burning tower. He killed the officers in the station. That's how he got out of the cell."

"Christ," one officer said, shaking his head. "Who would have thought he was capable of it?"

Rylie didn't say anything; she just gazed at Josh who now understood what she was doing. The only way that the town wouldn't believe in the spirits of Edward and Judith was if someone else was blamed for all the murders. It was breaking Rylie's heart, but it had to be done.

* * *

"So that's everything?" the sheriff asked as Rylie sat in his office with Josh.

"That's everything." She sniffed and wiped her eyes with the back of her hand. "It was Matt all along. I didn't want to . . . to believe it. But he was sick, not acting like himself."

"I'm very sorry, Rylie . . . sorry that you guys had to go through all of this," the sheriff said solemnly. "This is the worst massacre we've had in this town in two hundred years. I have to tell you, as sorry as I am that your brother was behind all of this, I'm glad the legend wasn't coming true. I was starting to believe it myself."

"I think we all were, sheriff," Josh said, rubbing Rylie's back as she wiped more tears from her eyes.

"Well, Rylie, your father should be here soon and your parents too, Josh," the sheriff said, standing up. "I'll want to talk to them all as well."

"Uh huh," Rylie said, rising from her chair.

"You two are free to go. Thank you again, Rylie, for telling me everything. I know it was hard."

Rylie forced a smile and walked out of the sheriff's office. Josh followed her out into the lobby where Andy, Brian, and Alec were waiting. They all stood up and the group walked out together. The color had finally returned to both Brian and Alec's faces since Luke's death.

Andy walked over to Rylie and pulled her into a tight hug. "I know that was hard." Andy sighed. "But this is the only way that it'll be over."

"I know," she said, trying to blink back tears. "And in the large scheme of things, it's a small price to pay for the safety of the townspeople. I just don't know how my dad is going to react."

As if on cue, her father burst into the police station and ran up to her. "Rylie, thank God." Andy let go of her and her father pulled her into a hug.

"Dad. . . ." She cried into his chest. "Dad, I'm so sorry."

"Don't be sorry, I'm just glad that you're okay," he said. She could see the pain on his face from the loss of his son.

"Mr. Bradford," the sheriff said as he opened the door to his office. "Can I speak with you for a little bit?"

"Sure, sheriff." He let go of Rylie and kissed her on the forehead. "I'll be back in a little bit and then we can go home."

"Home," she said, smiling as her father walked into the sheriff's office. "That word has never before sounded so good."

Chapter 12 – Forgetting

Rylie sat out in a stable stall on the soft hay and leaned back against Josh. He ran his hands up and down her arms. It had been over two weeks since the horrible events took place and they were finally feeling like normal kids again. Rylie glanced up at Josh and smiled. He leaned down and kissed her on the lips.

"You know, the whole time we've gone out, I think this is the first time we've been together to enjoy each other's company." Josh kissed her again.

"So you didn't enjoy my company any other time we hung out?" Rylie laughed.

"Oh, you know what I mean. Everything just seemed to go to hell after we started going out." He sighed and wrapped his arms around her. "And we haven't been alone that much. . . ."

"Yeah, I know what you mean," she said, placing her hands on his forearms. "But now we are alone and finally can be a normal teenage couple."

"Come on, Rylie, after everything we went through, I don't think we'll ever be normal again. What I saw. . . ." He stopped speaking when he saw the pain in her eyes returning. "Which I'm not going to talk about right now."

"No, Josh, it's fine. It's not like we can pretend it never happened. Everything's good now. The town's picking up the pieces and everybody's dealing with it."

"And how's your dad doing?" Josh asked daringly.

"Better than I thought he would be. Part of me thinks that he knows the truth, that he knows that it wasn't really Matt who killed all those people."

"You did explain to him at one point, and tried to get him to believe that Edward and Judith were behind the killings. Maybe your dad really did believe you after all."

159

"Maybe," she said. "This is not how I thought he would react to this situation."

"Give your dad some credit. He's probably a lot tougher than you think. More than anything, I think that he's glad that you're safe and sound."

"Yeah, I guess. Have you talked to Brian and Alec at all?"

"I talked to them yesterday; they seem almost like their normal selves again, which is really great. To see the two of them so blank and silent . . . it was weird."

"Well, that's good. Looks like everything is returning to normal, or as normal as it can be." She stood up and stretched in the growing dusk.

"Where are you going?" he asked, climbing to his feet.

"I told you earlier, today is the day that we finally let go for good." She walked over to where the saddles were hanging on the wall and picked up her bag off one of the hooks.

"And that is supposed to mean . . . ?"

"Just follow me," she said, taking his hand as she slung the bag over her shoulder.

"Fine." they walked out of the stables and down toward the edge of the woods.

It was a little over two weeks ago that she and Josh had found the dead cows here. She tried to shake that image away, but she knew she would never be completely rid of those images. They would always be in her mind no matter how much therapy she went to or how much she tried to block them from her memory.

Josh seemed to be thinking the same thing as they crossed over into the woods and walked into a small clearing where Andy was starting the bonfire. He was stoking the fire as they walked up to him and Rylie set her bag on the ground next to a log.

"This is a nice spot back here. It'd be great for parties," Josh said.

"It's strange to think about normal teenage stuff like parties and school again, isn't it?" Rylie commented.

"Sure is," Andy said. "You brought everything, right?"

"Yep," Rylie said, opening her bag.

"What exactly are we doing here? You said that we were letting go," Josh said, confused.

"We're getting rid of all the evidence for good," she said, pulling out the spell book, Mary's diary, the amulet, and the piece of paper that the spell was on.

She hesitated for a second before throwing it all onto the fire. It didn't take long for the flames to reduce everything to ash. The darkness grew around them.

"Now there's no chance of anyone knowing the truth. The only thing left of Mary, Edward, and Judith is the legend in the museum . . . and a skewed legend at that," Rylie said.

"That's good, right?" Andy asked. "Most of the people who believe in Bloody Friday will have it all wrong."

"It's very good. The legend is never going to go away, but it's better to know the lie rather than the truth. In this case, ignorance really is bliss," she said sadly. She was thinking of Matt, who they buried four days prior. "I can tell you one thing; this will be the last year that I celebrate Bloody Friday."

"Thank God," Andy said emphatically.

"It's so crazy to think that tomorrow is just going to be a regular Monday at school," Josh commented.

161

"Everything had to go back to the everyday swing of things at some point." Andy sighed as he sat down on one of the logs. "Normal sounds really good to me."

"Yeah, it does." Rylie sat down next to him.

"So does anyone know a good ghost story?" Andy asked jokingly.

"Andy, I swear to God." Rylie smacked him on the arm, causing him to fall back a bit on the log.

"Hey, watch it," he said, laughing.

"I'll be happy if I never hear a ghost story as long as I live," Josh said. "What do you say we go and get some dinner like normal teenagers?"

"Sounds like an excellent idea," Andy said, getting up and throwing a bucket of water over the flames.

"Let me just run up to the house and clean up a bit," Rylie said as they started out of the dark woods and up to the house.

They walked across the front lawn and up to the front porch where her dad was sitting on the swing looking across the fields at the horizon. It was clear that her father was grieving, but he seemed to be handling it well. Josh and Andy walked toward Andy's truck, giving her space to talk to her father if she chose to.

"Hey, Dad," Rylie said. She sat next to him on the swing.

"Hey, Rye." He turned and smiled at her.

"Josh, Andy, and I are going out to grab some dinner. Can we get you anything?"

"No, I'm fine. There are leftovers from the countless casseroles that people left us," he reminded her.

"I never really got that. It's like people think the casseroles will make everything better," Rylie said.

"It's their way of saying sorry and that they're here for us."

"And nothing says it like a green bean casserole," she said, giggling. Her father couldn't resist chuckling.

"You guys have fun. But don't stay out to late. I want you home by ten. It's a school night," he reminded her.

"School—I had almost forgotten about it."

"I know it's been a rough week," he said. "But the school year's almost over and then summer will be here."

"That's one way to look at it."

"Tell Josh that I expect to see him at conditioning tomorrow night. Just because he's dating my daughter doesn't mean he gets a free pass." He smiled, and that made Rylie smile even more.

That was the first time he had acknowledged that she and Josh were going out without making a face. "I'll let him know."

She walked upstairs to her room and quickly changed to a nice blouse. She touched up her makeup and pulled part of the front of her hair back with bobby pins. She smiled at herself in the mirror, grabbed her purse from off her dresser, and started out of her room. Something she saw in the mirror stopped her. For a moment, fear gripped her.

She slowly backed up to look at the mirror and her heart flip-flopped as she saw Mary standing behind her, dressed in her usual long green dress. She was standing there smiling at Rylie. The expression on Mary's face put Rylie at ease as she stared back at the spirit through the mirror. Rylie glanced behind her but saw no one there. She turned back to the mirror to see that Mary had moved closer to her.

Mary seemed to be wearing the amulet and this made Rylie happy; it was in good hands. Edward and Judith would never get out again. Mary extended her hand and placed it on Rylie's shoulder. Coldness crept into every part of Rylie's body, but it was almost comforting. Rylie knew that this was Mary's way of saying thanks.

"No problem, Mary," Rylie said aloud. "It was all for the greater good. I should be thanking you. It was you who pointed me in all the right directions. I hope you can rest in peace now."

Mary nodded and faded away, leaving nothing but the coldness that still gripped Rylie. She turned and walked down the stairs and out the front door. She said goodbye to her father one more time and gave him a kiss on the cheek. Then she walked over to the truck and climbed in along with Josh and Andy.

Josh put his hand on her shoulder, in the same place that Mary had touched her. He withdrew it quickly. "Why are you so cold?" Fear flashed across his eyes.

"Mary paid me a little visit," Rylie explained.

"I thought we were done with all those spirits," Andy said as he started the truck.

"She was just saying thanks and bye," Rylie said.

"Well, thank God," Josh said, relieved.

"Mary was never evil. She was the one that helped us out, remember?"

"Yeah, I remember, but spirits just don't sit well with me," Josh said.

"Josh, I promise it's over." Rylie took his hand as they drove through the woods into town.

164

They rolled along until they got into town and Andy parked in the parking lot near the school. Rylie felt strange being back in town; she had only been here once since that night.

The three of them walked along the road toward the Italian restaurant. The road was bustling with people now; it was a far cry from the deserted town that they had witnessed that night. Once everyone found out that Matt killed all those people, they had all come back to town. The museum was being fixed up and so was the police station and the library.

The only thing that was left as a reminder of that night was the half of a clock tower that lingered in the center of town. Rylie stared at it as they walked along and swallowed hard. She could remember being up in that tower as if it were yesterday. Josh saw the look on her face and he put his arm around her waist in comfort as they walked. Andy, who had come to terms with the two of them together, still rolled his eyes in annoyance.

"Rylie!" a female voice called.

Rylie stopped and turned. Sarah was running toward her. She ran up to her and threw her arms around Rylie, hugging her tightly.

"I heard what happened," she said as she let her go. "I'm so sorry, Rye, I wish I had been here."

"I'm glad you weren't here. One less person that didn't have to witness what we witnessed," Rylie said sadly.

"What exactly happened? I saw the clock tower but even Chris didn't seem to know exactly what happened. There are a million stories floating around."

"Sarah, it's a really long story," Rylie said, sighing.

"At some point, you're going to have to tell me all of it," she said, putting her arm around her as they walked to the restaurant behind Andy and Josh. "First, you have to fill me in on why I just saw Josh's hand wrapped around your waist."

"And that is another long story." Rylie slipped out from under Sarah's arm and walked backward down the street.

"Rylie Bradford, you have got to tell me!" Sarah exclaimed.

"All in due time, my friend," Rylie promised, smiling widely.

"I swear, you are so frustrating," Sarah retorted.

"And you are still friends with me," Rylie said, sticking her tongue out.

Brian and Alec were sitting at a table near the back; they called to Josh and Andy. Rylie and Sarah made their way over and they pulled a couple of tables together.

"Chris should be coming too," Sarah said.

"Great, the gang's all here," Rylie replied.

Josh came up from behind her and put his arms around her. "See, I told you things were going back to the way they were," Josh whispered in her ear as everyone else sat down at the table.

"Actually that's not true," she said.

"What do you mean? Because of what happened before we left?"

"No, that's not what I mean. Things are better than they were before, because now I have you."

"That is true, and I do think that you look very good with me on you."

"Oh, really now? I think it's the other way around," she said, smiling up at him. He kissed her lightly on the mouth.

166

The two of them then sat down, ordered pizza, and chatted the night away like nothing had ever happened. It was as if the events that they had witnessed were tucked away and weren't going to surface for a long time. It was exactly that way Rylie wanted it to be.

Epilogue

"Craig, what are we doing here?" Madison asked her boyfriend as she pointed the flashlight up the stairs of the clock tower.

"Come on; stop being a scaredy-cat. Everyone's waiting." Craig smiled playfully as they walked up the stairs.

"If my mom and dad find out that I snuck out of my house at midnight, they're going to ground me," she said as they reached the landing.

"They're not going to find out; I'll make sure of it."

"Fine." She sighed.

They walked over to their circle of friends. Someone had lit candles all along the floor of the tower. Two of their friends were sipping beers; the others were holding paper cups.

"Guys, if we get caught. . . ." Madison started.

"Come on, Maddie, you really need to lighten up," Trent said, laughing.

"With friends like you, it's not easy," she said, though a smile crossed her lips.

"Just sit down and grab a beer," Trent said.

The two of them joined the rest. Trent tossed them both beers and Madison reluctantly opened hers and took a swig. Her eyes scanned the dark tower where the only lights came from the dancing flames of the candles.

"Craig, what are we doing here again?" Trent asked. "Besides having a good time…"

"You guys know where we are, right?" Craig grinned as he took a swig of beer

"The clock tower; so what?" Kristen flipped her blonde hair over her slender shoulder.

"You guys know what happened here five years ago?" he asked.

"That guy went on a rampage. His family still owns a farm in the west end."

"Pretty much, yeah. He killed a whole bunch of people in the town within three days. He was psychotic or something," Craig explained. "He trashed the museum, slaughtered three cops when they tried to put him into a holding cell. . . ."

"Shit, man." Trent leaned back and sipped his beer. "So why are we in the tower? Did something happen here?"

"This is where he died, remember?" Craig finished his beer in one gulp. "He lured his own sister up here to kill her, but her boyfriend saved her. That's when he torched the tower before jumping out."

A look of recognition dawned on Kristen. "Oh, right, and then they decided to rebuild this tower two years ago."

"And some say that the ghost of Matt still haunts the tower," Craig added.

"And who says that?" Madison asked incredulously.

"You know, people in town," Craig said ominously.

"It's an urban legend," Madison said, rolling her eyes. "That probably isn't even the real story. These stories change over the years to fit with the times, but they're not real."

"Well, okay, sorry," Craig retorted. "But that didn't stop you from being scared to come up here tonight."

"This whole thing is stupid. What did you expect? Did you think you were going to see a ghost?" Madison asked. "I just didn't want to get in trouble, that's all."

"Calm down. It's just something fun to do in this stupid town," Craig said. "We thought we'd spice it up a little."

"I thought at least one of us would get lucky tonight," Trent said, laughing.

"You guys are pigs," Madison said. "Come on, Craig, let's go."

"We just got here, I don't want to go."

"Fine. You guys can stay here and drink your beer and wait for that ghost to show up." Madison climbed to her feet. "I'm out of here."

She walked passed the opening in the tower and jumped because she thought she saw someone sitting there. She stopped and stared at the opening, but there was nothing there. She shook her head and continued to walk toward the stairs. When she reached the bottom, she heard someone running up behind her. She turned around to see Craig.

"Madison, don't go. Look, I'm sorry about what Trent said. He's an ass."

"At least we can agree on one thing." She started to laugh, but then she glanced up at the tower, gasped, and jumped back.

Flames leapt around the tower. Through the flames, she saw a strange symbol that she had never seen before. Craig touched her shoulders and glanced at her worriedly.

"Madison, are you okay?"

"The tower," she stammered, looking at him and then back at the building.

"What about it?"

Madison blinked. There was nothing there. The tower looked as it always had. "I *um*. . . I thought I saw something."

"Look, babe, you were right; that story was just an urban legend. It's not real."

"I know that, but I just. . . I guess I'm just tired."

"Maybe I should take you home."

She smiled mischievously and ran her fingers along his chest. "We could go back to your place instead."

"My parents aren't back from their trip yet. The house is empty."

"I know that." All she wanted to do at the moment was to push the image of what she had seen out of her mind. "But I think Trent was right. Someone's getting lucky tonight."

"I like the way you talk," Craig said as he put his arm around her shoulder.

They walked down the street and Madison tried with all her will to keep from looking back at the tower. Despite herself, she turned and looked back, then breathed a sigh of relief. The tower was intact—no flames, no splintering wood. She smiled, but the smile faded fast as the odd symbol appeared on the side of the tower. She turned back around as they continued to walk.

"Maddie, you okay?" Craig asked.

"Yeah, I'm fine. Let's just hurry, okay?"

"Yeah, sure." Craig glanced back at the tower one last time as they walked along the dark road. He had a sinking feeling in his stomach that he should've never taken Madison into that tower.

www.ingramcontent.com/pod-product-compliance
Lightning Source LLC
Chambersburg PA
CBHW050945120626
46552CB00001B/397